Rivers to Blood

Books by Michael Lister

(John Jordan novels)
Power in the Blood
Blood of the Lamb
Flesh and Blood
The Body and the Blood
Blood Sacrifice
Rivers to Blood

(Short Story Collections)
North Florida Noir
Florida Heat Wave
Delta Blues
Another Quiet Night in Desparation

(Remington James novels)
Double Exposure
Separation Anxiety

(Merrick McKnight novels)
Thunder Beach
A Certain Retribution

(Jimmy "Soldier" Riley novels)
The Big Goodbye
The Big Beyond
The Big Hello

(Sam Michaels and Daniel Davis Series)
Burnt Offerings
Separation Anxiety

(The Meaning Series)
The Meaning of Jesus
Meaning Every Moment
The Meaning of Life in Movies
The Meaning of Life

Rivers to Blood
Michael Lister

a John Jordan novel

You buy a book. We plant a tree.

Inquiries should be addressed to:
Pulpwood Press
P.O. Box 35038
Panama City, FL 32412

Lister, Michael.
Rivers to Blood / Michael
Lister.
-----1st ed.
p. cm.

ISBN: 978-1-888146-39-4   Hardcover

ISBN: 978-1-888146--40-0   Paperback

Library of Congress Control Number:

Book Design by Adam Ake

Printed in the United States

1 3 5 7 9 10 8 6 4 2

First Edition

For Dawn and our crew:

Dave Lloyd
Aaron Bearden
Suz Windham
DeDe Mohr
Herbie Lawley
Tony Buoni
Lynn Wallace
Margaret Webster
Kenny, Chelsey, and Zander Ardire

Thank You
Dawn, Jill, Amy, Adam

Chapter One

I was almost home when it happened.

I had taken the day off, and after mowing the grass between downpours had driven into Panama City to spend the afternoon browsing its bookstores. The pollen I stirred while cutting the grass and the dust I dislodged while deshelving the books had kicked my allergies into overdrive, and I felt dizzy and disconnected as I drove down the long, mostly empty stretch of pine-tree-lined highway toward Pottersville.

It was early August in one of the hottest and wettest summers on record. Severe thunderstorms—sometimes several in a day—were followed by a full-on assault of the sun, steam rising from earth and asphalt creating sauna-like conditions, intense and inescapable.

North Florida summers alternate between parched and drenched. There is rarely anything in between.

I was listening to a book on the fabric of the cosmos, straining my allergy-addled brain to understand some of the current concepts, when I passed the van. I didn't pay much attention to it, but instinctively glanced in my rearview to see if it bore a yellow DC license plate.

It did.

Since becoming the chaplain of Potter Correctional Institution, I had begun to pay close attention to white vans on the highway, knowing the ones with yellow Department of

Corrections tags were transporting inmates. Like all activities that took inmates outside the institution, transporting them— whether to the hospital, courthouse, or on funeral furlough— was not only when most escapes were attempted but when most attempted were successful.

It is extremely difficult for inmates to escape from a Florida state prison. There are just too many barriers—too many locked doors and gates, too many staff, too much chain link and razor wire—but once outside, the barriers decrease dramatically.

Four electronically locked gates become one van door. Fifty officers backed up by a riot squad become two officers— only one of which has a gun.

I'm not saying it's easy for an inmate to escape while on transport—he's still in cuffs, shackles, and a belly chain connecting the two with a black box covering the lock—just that it's easier.

When I realized my wandering mind had missed the last several lines of the book, I paused it. As I did, I glanced in my mirror again to see that the van was nearly out of sight.

It had stopped raining for the moment, but my back window was still dotted with raindrops, clouds were blocking out much of the afternoon sun, and a low-lying mist just above the road and ditches made seeing much of anything more than a little challenging.

Yet that's when I saw it. Or thought I did.

Brake lights. The van swerving. Maybe even running off the road.

It was possible I was being paranoid.

I could've just imagined the whole thing, projected what I was looking for onto the faint raindrop-spotted image, but I had to turn around to find out for sure.

I slowed and pulled off onto the soft, soggy shoulder of the road, water sloshing beneath my tires, leaving black tracks in the wet grass behind me as I eased back on the highway heading in the opposite direction.

Depending on an inmate's custody level, there are different requirements related to transport. Close custody and close management inmates have to be cuffed and shackled and escorted by two armed officers. A single unarmed officer can escort a work camp inmate, and the inmate doesn't even have to be cuffed.

Most often, however, there were two officers involved. Both sat in the front of the van, separated from the inmate or inmates—there could be as few as one and as many as thirteen—by a metal mesh and plexiglass partition. In the back, inmates were often cuffed and shackled, but never chained to the vehicle. The windows of the van were fitted with expanded metal reinforcements that looked like large blinds, and both the back and side doors were padlocked with hasps welded on the outside.

I raced back down the highway as fast as I could, the frame of my old truck shaking under the strain.

Tall grass and weeds filled the shoulders of the road, the seed heads of Bahia stalks glistening even in the low light of the overcast afternoon. Sprouting out of the shoots periodically, mostly next to signposts, rain-streaked and leaning political signs announced the vast number of Potter county citizens who aspired to public office, while water flowed through the drainage ditches like rushing rivers.

Several of the signs lining the side of the road bore my name, and it was disconcerting to see. I wasn't the John Jordan running for reelection as Potter County Sheriff, my dad was, and though most if not all citizens knew that, I still felt embarrassed at having my name splattered all over the county.

Squinting, scanning, searching.

Looking for lights, movement, anything.

The only ones I saw were from a vehicle in the distance heading toward me. The bright headlights made it difficult to see anything else, and I had to wait until the gap between us closed and we passed each other before I could start looking for the van again.

There was nothing on the road in front of me now. Not even a random oncoming car. And the long, flat road seemed to stretch out forever.

Then, just ahead, near the entrance to a dirt road that angled back off the highway into the woods, I saw skid marks that continued onto the shoulder, becoming tracks on the narrow, muddy, hole-pocked road.

I followed them.

Chapter Two

The narrow dirt road was dark, the thick canopy of branches, leaves, and Spanish moss blocking out what little light the cloudy evening offered.

It wound back through the woods toward the river.

Most likely used for logging many years ago, now the road mostly provided access to the woods for hunters in the winter and to the river for fishermen in the summer.

The skid marks back on the highway could have been made at any time, but with all the water that had washed over the dirt road this afternoon, I knew the tracks I was now following were fresh.

The woods surrounding me on all sides were dense and ropy with a seemingly infinite variety of shades of green, every raindrop-dappled leaf glistening in the glare of my headlights as if freshly formed.

I drove faster than I should have under the current conditions, my truck bouncing through the mud-filled potholes, each bump staining my white truck the color of heavily creamed coffee. Sliding from side to side, the back end fishtailing, I almost lost control of the vehicle several times, but when I saw lights up ahead, I sped up even more.

The road twisted and turned often, sharp curves at odd angles shortening the sight line to nearly nonexistent.

On one particularly tricky turn, I almost drove straight

off the road and into the woods, and as I came through it, I realized that's exactly what the van had done.

And that's when I did it.

Without thinking, I jerked my foot off the gas and stomped on the brake. The truck began a hydroplane that spun it around several times before it flipped over twice and slammed into the base of a thick-bodied pine tree.

It happened so fast I didn't fully realize what had happened until I found myself hanging upside down, suspended by my seatbelt in the overturned truck.

I took a moment to move around as best I could to see if anything hurt. It didn't. I pressed the seatbelt button and I fell head first onto the roof of my cab. Now it did.

As I carefully crawled over the broken glass and through the passenger window, I could feel tremors beginning to run the length of my body. Stumbling to my feet, I stood for a moment on wobbly legs wishing I had a weapon.

Slowly and stiffly I began to walk back toward the curve and the new path the van had cut into the thicket.

The van had missed the curve, driven some thirty feet into the woods, and smashed into an enormous old oak tree.

The engine was off, but the vehicle's headlights were still on, their beams refracting a million raindrops, making the sequined forest shimmer and sparkle in a way that seemed almost magical.

All of the van's doors were closed and there was no movement. I approached from the rear on the driver's side slowly, looking over my shoulder often, but stopped when I heard a small plane overhead.

The engine of the plane seemed to be straining, alternating between a high-pitched whine and cutting out altogether. It sounded to me as if the aircraft were falling from the sky, though I couldn't be sure.

I looked up for confirmation.

At first I couldn't see anything, but as the sound grew louder, I actually thought the plane might be about to crash right on top of me.

When I finally caught sight of it again, it was headed down fast at an angle that left little doubt it was about to crash.

Another moment and I heard what sounded like the plane scraping across the tops of trees, but was momentarily distracted by a noise behind me.

As I started to turn, I was hit in the back of the head by a heavy object swung with furious force.

I lost consciousness before I hit the ground.

Chapter Three

When I opened my eyes, the first thing I saw was the van.

I scrambled to my feet, the back of my head throbbing, wondering how long I had been out.

Not long from the look of things.

Though it was difficult to judge on such an overcast day, it didn't seem to be much later.

Glancing around for my assailant, I made my way over to the van.

Kent Murphy, the middle-aged transport officer, was slumped in the driver's seat unconscious, his light brown CO shirt soaked with blood.

The passenger seat and the back of the van were empty.

I carefully opened the door and felt for a pulse.

He had one. Weak, but there.

I reached across him, getting blood on my shirt, grabbed the mic, and radioed the institution, describing for them the situation as best I could with the few 10-codes I knew. I wasn't sure they understood everything, but 10-20, 10-33, and 10-71 let them know where I was, that it was an emergency, and to send an ambulance.

I couldn't decide if I should move Kent, so left him as he was.

It should take the ambulance less than ten minutes to arrive. While waiting, I went around to the other side of the van.

Both the front and side doors were closed and the side door was still padlocked, which meant the inmate being transported should still be inside. Cupping my hands around my face, I pressed up against the glass to search the back of the van. All the seats were empty. Moving around and looking from various angles, I could see that the floorboard was too.

It was possible there had never actually been an inmate inside. Kent could have been returning from dropping one off or on his way to pick one up—but then who hit me in the back of the head?

I was on my way around the van to check on Kent again when I heard the noise.

It sounded like faint moaning, and it was coming from the woods out from the passenger side of the van. Stepping over thick undergrowth and fallen branches, and hoping I wouldn't step on a rattlesnake, I began to move in the direction of the sound.

The woods were still, the only movement raindrops falling from treetops. Crickets, convinced by the dark storm clouds that it was night, chirped loudly, but the sky was clearing up, the light beneath the pines slowly increasing.

It didn't take long to find him.

Lying facedown, his blue inmate uniform wet, a white guy with reddish-blond hair with traces of blood in it was moving slightly and moaning, as if experiencing a bad dream.

I was really confused now.

I had expected to find an officer, not an inmate. How did he get out of the locked van? Who hit him on the back of the head? The same person who hit me? But why? I had figured it was an inmate trying to escape. And maybe it was. Maybe there were two or more. But that didn't explain how they got out of the locked van. And why leave one behind? Perhaps he wanted to stay. An inmate with a low custody level and very little time left on his sentence had no reason to run. And with no cuffs or leg irons, it was likely he was a low custody, little time, work camp inmate. Maybe the other inmate or inmates knocked him out to keep him quiet for their escape. Maybe he tried to stop them.

Hearing sirens out on the highway, I turned to watch for their approach.

Dad arrived first. Alone in his truck.

"John," Dad yelled.

He was followed by two of his deputies, an ambulance, and several officers from the prison.

"Over here," I yelled back. "Kent Murphy's in the van. He's in bad shape. Tell them to treat him first. And I've got an inmate down over here who needs to be looked at."

"You okay?"

"Yeah."

"Anyone else?"

"Be careful," I said. "Somebody whacked me on the back of the head. Maybe this guy too."

Taking charge, Dad began giving orders, directing his deputies to sweep the area, the EMTs to treat Kent, and the correctional officers to find out exactly who had been in the van.

A few moments later, Dad and I were leaning against his vehicle while the EMTs worked on Kent and the inmate, while the correctional officers and deputies searched the woods around us.

If all the signs on the side of the road didn't announce that it was an election year, the way Dad was dressed would. Ordinarily a casually dressed sheriff, Jack Jordan, for the past several months, and foreseeable future, was wearing blazers and ties—and judging from how stylish he looked, I'd guess he had a new girlfriend helping him shop.

"What happened?" he asked.

I told him, pressing the ice pack one of the EMTs gave me to the growing knot on the back of my head as I did.

"How bad's your truck?" he asked.

"Totaled," I said.

"It was time for a new one anyway."

"It's been time," I said. "That was never the issue."

His expression let me know he wondered what the issue was. Though he rarely said much about it, Dad did not approve of a lot of what I did—spending what little money I made on books and helping AA buddies instead of buying decent transportation and living accommodations, being a chaplain instead of a cop, and for generally being different from him in nearly every way.

"How goes the campaign?" I asked.

He shook his head and frowned. "Not good."

After several decades of running for reelection with little or no opposition, there were nearly ten men in the race for sheriff this time. I wasn't sure why—I had little use for politics, local or otherwise—but I knew enough to know that so many candidates meant one thing. The perception was Dad was vulnerable.

"You got a new girlfriend?" I asked.

"Who told you that?"

"Just wondered."

I could see it dawning on him. He looked down at what he was wearing and smiled appreciatively.

A car pulled up behind the last vehicle, and the OIC from the prison jumped out and ran over to us. Captain Tom McGlon was on the young side of middle age, with strawberry-blond hair and fair skin with a reddish hue and a light dusting of pale freckles.

"Got confirmation," he said. "Two transport officers—Kent Murphy and Allen Pettis—and one work camp inmate were in the van."

I took off running toward the inmate.

"What is it?" Dad asked.

He and Tom fell in right behind me.

"You know what Pettis looks like?" I asked Tom.

"Yeah," he said. "Why?"

"Because," I said, "the man in the inmate uniform might be him."

Chapter Four

With Kent Murphy on his way to the hospital, the recently revived Allen Pettis, still wearing the inmate uniform, was about to tell us what had happened.

I had discarded my ice pack, but he still held his tightly against the back of his head.

"I think he hit me harder than he hit you, Chaplain," he said.

"More likely his head's harder," Tom McGlon said. "What happened?"

"Kent and me was takin' a inmate back to the work camp. He'd been at the main unit for medical. We didn't have him cuffed or nothin'."

Like many of the people in Pottersville, Allen Pettis wasn't nearly as ignorant or uneducated as he sounded. He simply had poor grammar—like so many of the teachers who taught him in school.

"He never gave us any trouble before," Pettis continued. "He was a good inmate. Hell, he can't have much time left."

"I pulled his file before I came over," Tom said. "He's minimum custody and got less than three months left on his sentence. He's in on a small non-violent drug charge."

"Well he's picked up a few new tricks since he's been inside," Pettis said, rubbing his head.

"I've got to get the dogs out here," Tom said, looking around the woods at the COs and deputies searching the area.

"Anyway," Pettis continued, "they's a section of plexiglass missin' from the cage in the van. It's right behind the driver's seat. The metal mesh is there, but the plexiglass don't reach all the way." Looking up at Tom, he added, "I told maintenance about it just a few days ago." He then paused long enough to shake his head before he continued. "We's drivin' down the highway, not payin' attention to much of nothin', when the inmate slipped a piece of wire through the cage and around Kent's neck and began to choke him. He told him to pull off the road and for me to unlock the van and let him out or he'd kill him. Murphy lost control and we wound up out here. The wreck knocked Kent unconscious, but the inmate was still going to kill him if I didn't let him out, so I unlocked the door, thinkin' I could jump him when he come out, but he got the better of me. I'm sorry. I . . . I should've . . . but I couldn't let Kent die. I done the best I could."

"Why the hell would an inmate with so little time left escape now?" Tom asked.

"You just can't never tell about no damn inmate," Pettis said. "If they had any sense they wouldn't be in prison in the first place."

"Could be any number of reasons," I said, "but news he got at his medical appointment is probably a good place to start."

Tom snatched the radio off his belt and pressed the call button. When the control room responded, he said. "Where the hell's my K-9 officer?"

"We're trying to locate him now, sir," the control room sergeant said. "He's not answering his cell phone or pages."

"He's probably with search and rescue on the river," Dad said. "That's where Jake is."

That reminded me of what I saw right before I was knocked out. I had forgotten until now.

"Did the plane go into the river?" I asked.

"What plane?" Dad asked.

"Just before I was knocked out," I said. "There was a plane overhead. I thought it might be crashing."

"They're doing training exercises. Think we'd've heard by now if there was a plane crash."

"I could have sworn it was going to crash," I said.

"You think you can get Jake on the radio?" Tom said to Dad.

He nodded.

"Come on," Dad then said to me. "Let's ride over to the landing and see if we can find 'em. I'll radio Jake on the way." He looked at Tom. "In the meantime, I'll get some more men out here to help search. See if you can too."

Chapter Five

Dad's truck was immaculate inside and out, except for the fresh mud on the tires, fenders, and quarter panels, and I knew it was because inmates from the jail cleaned it daily. Perhaps because of the extra scrutiny that comes in an election year, there was nothing personal in the vehicle except for the stacks of campaign cards, brochures, and door hangers in the backseat.

"How's your mother?" he asked.

Though they had been divorced longer than they were together, he still always asked me about her—especially since she had been diagnosed with cirrhosis of the liver.

I shook my head. "Doesn't have much longer."

"You've been saying that a while now."

"She's lasted a lot longer than any of us thought she would—including her doctor," I said, "but . . ."

Mom was hanging on for some reason. I just didn't know what it was. I suspected it had to do with Jake not being ready or her holding out hope that she might be reconciled with my sister Nancy before she died.

"Need to go by and see her," he said.

I loved my dad, respected him in a lot of ways, but I couldn't help but wonder if part of the reason for his visit was to take her an absentee ballot. He knew she would sign it. She'd do anything for him—anything but the one thing he wanted her to. She wouldn't stop drinking. Not even for him.

"You got any sense how the prison will vote?"

I shook my head.

Of all the different things my dad was, I liked the politician the least.

"Wish we could find out," he said.

The prison vote, like the black vote or the women's vote, was not monolithic, had never been a solid block, but that didn't keep many politicians from believing it was. No one candidate would get the entire prison vote—not even the correctional officer who was running.

"The ones who say anything are going to act like they're for you to my face," I said, "but you can't go on that."

He nodded. "I know."

"You really think it's going to be that close?" I asked.

"I think if it was today, I'd lose."

That surprise me—both that he thought it and that he said it. No one had ever come close to beating him before.

"Really?"

He nodded again.

"Why?"

"There's just too many running," he said. "We're going to split up the vote so many ways it won't take many to win. I've done some unpopular things over the years, made the wrong enemies. Hell, one of my own deputies is running against me."

I nodded, but didn't say anything, and he tried to radio Jake again.

Fred Goodwin, the deputy running for sheriff, was one of the most active members of the volunteer search and rescue, and I wondered if that was the reason Dad was driving over to the landing himself instead of sending one of his deputies.

I thought he'd had a specific reason relating to the escape for asking me to join him, but now suspected it was just for company and to talk politics.

I'd much rather be back in the woods helping search for the escaped inmate and getting my truck towed.

"Wonder what really made him run?" Dad said.

"Who?" I asked, wondering if he were talking about one of his political challengers.

"The inmate."

I shrugged.

"Had to be something big," he said.

"Probably, but not necessarily," I said. "It may not be logical at all. I've known inmates with less time than him run because they said they couldn't do even one more minute— much less several days."

He nodded. "True. But most have a better reason than that."

"If it's something significant we should be able to find out what it is."

"When you find out will you let me know first?" he asked.

He was assuming that I would look into it, which was not unreasonable, and he had asked me to keep him informed about investigations in the prison before, but he had never asked me to tell him something I discovered first. Of course, he had never been facing such a close election before either.

I lied and said I would.

Chapter Six

Formed from the joining of the Chattahoochee and Flint rivers, the 106-mile-long Apalachicola River flows from the Jim Woodruff Dam near Chattahoochee to dump sixteen billion gallons of fresh water into the Apalachicola Bay every day. Mixing with the salt water of the Gulf, the fresh water of the river creates a rich estuarine system for many species of marine life, including the best-tasting oysters in the world.

Continually a source of controversy, the Apalachicola River is constantly facing issues related to dredging, Navy SEALs training, and freshwater flow levels because of having upstream waters diverted to Atlanta or Alabama. But none of this can detract from the fact that its banks hold some of the most spectacular scenery in all of Florida—a state known for its natural beauty.

Dad and I were standing at the river's edge in silence, waiting for the Potter County Search and Rescue team to arrive. When we had finally gotten Jake on the radio, he said they would return to the landing as fast as they could, but that it wouldn't be fast.

Potter County Search and Rescue is a small not-for-profit group of specially trained volunteers who search for missing persons. The highly skilled agency specializes in dark water recovery of lost, abducted, or drowning victims, and is comprised mostly of local law enforcement, mainly off-duty deputies and correctional officers, a few citizen volunteers rounding out the tight-knit team. Since most of their time is spent searching for people who vanish while on the river, they spend a lot of time training here.

Because it was a weekday and the weather was so rainy, the landing was empty, its parking lot devoid of the usual pickup trucks and SUVs and empty boat trailers, its playground missing the laughter and shrieks of children, its picnic pavilions not providing cover for birthday parties and family reunions, its built-in grills and cooking areas failing to fill the area with the aroma of hamburgers and hotdogs being chargrilled or fresh fish frying like it did on pretty weather weekends and holidays.

By the time the search and rescue boat rounded the bend in the river just above us, the clouds had cleared and the late afternoon sun was far brighter than the early afternoon one had been. The search and rescue boat, like most of the group's equipment, had been purchased with the proceeds of fundraisers like the annual fishing tournament it sponsored. It was large, holding not only the young paramilitary men in their various poses, but all their dive gear and rescue equipment as well.

We walked down the aluminum gangplank to the floating wooden dock to meet them. Fred Goodwin, the silver-haired sixty-something-year-old detective from Dad's department who was running against him, pulled the boat up beside the dock.

"It must be a sure enough emergency to get the sheriff out of his office," Goodwin said.

The tension between Dad and Goodwin was palpable, and the search and rescue guys seemed nervous and uncomfortable, as if confused by conflicting loyalties and cross-purpose allegiances.

Ignoring Goodwin, Jake said, "How'd he escape? John let 'im go?"

Dad told them.

The bottom of the wide boat was littered with duffle

bags and dive gear, and Shane Bryant, Todd Sears, and Sandy
Hartman, the three COs from the prison, busied themselves
gathering up the equipment and cleaning up as they listened.

As Dad spoke, I studied the small group of men.
With the exception of Sandy, they all shared the Southern
good ol' bad boy traits of tough-guy posturing, folksy anti-
intellectualism, covert racism, and general xenophobia.

Shane and Todd, and to a little lesser extent, Jake, looked
like they belonged on the SAR team—young, athletic, muscular.
The others did not. Sandy was too soft, Fred too old, and
Kenny Bateson too fat.

When Dad finished, he said, "We need to get the dogs
over there as soon as possible."

Todd continued gathering up his things. He was good
with the dogs, great at tracking down inmates, but he didn't like
being told what to do and Dad had no direct authority over
him. He was going to take his time gathering up his things and
go when he got ready.

I said, "You guys see a small plane? Sounded like it was
having engine trouble."

Jake said, "What's that got to do with the escape? You
think he hopped a plane?"

"Did it crash?" I asked.

"Yeah," Kenny said, "and we're over here shootin' the
shit with you."

He was a loud, obnoxious man with darkly tanned, sun-
damaged skin, and an enormous belly that hung down over his
faded and frayed cutoff blue jeans. He rarely wore a shirt or
shoes, and he was the only non law enforcement member of the
team present.

"We didn't get a good look at it," Todd said, "but I think
we'd a heard if it went down."

Kenny was the only member of the group who was
excessively obese and looked out of place. A few of the others
carried a little extra beer weight, but Todd and Shane were

bodybuilders, spending several hours a day in the weight room at the prison or high school—and they wore too-small shirts that showed off all their work.

As usual, Sandy had yet to say anything. Quiet, sensitive, and slightly effeminate, he was nearly the opposite of the other members of the team, and probably would not be tolerated if he weren't by far the best diver in the area.

"I could have sworn it was going to crash when I saw it," I said.

"When was that?" Goodwin asked.

"Just before I was knocked out," I said.

"Knocked out?" Todd Sears said.

"Convict sapped him with an oak limb," Dad said.

Jake laughed. "Bet crashing planes weren't all you saw."

"Well," Goodwin said, "I think we'd all know it if it went down, but if it'd make you feel better, we can take you back up the river to look for it—if it's okay with the sheriff."

Dad sighed and nodded. "Look for the inmate while you're at it. He may try to cross. Todd, you get the dogs and meet me back at the scene."

"Sure thing, boss," Goodwin said.

"Let me get my gear first," Todd said.

"It can't wait?" Dad asked, his impatience obvious.

"No," Todd said, "it can't."

"Well hurry. He's got a big jump on us already."

"Oh, I'll catch the convict," Todd said. "Needn't worry 'bout that. Never had one get away yet."

"You boys make some room for the chaplain," Goodwin said.

As Dad left and Todd finished what he was doing, the boys gathered up their duffle bags and dive gear, quickly shuffled it off the boat and into their jacked-up and bulldogged trucks.

I shot them a quizzical look. "What if we need that?"

"It's just our empty tanks and some random dive gear,"

Goodwin said. "There's more on the boat."

The others rejoined us. Todd shoved us away from the dock and Goodwin gunned the engine. Within moments the bow of the boat was raised and we were racing down the river, the setting sun starting to streak the horizon with flamingo feathers.

"Any idea where we should look?" Goodwin yelled over the wind and motor.

I told him.

For several hours, we searched the area the plane was most likely to have gone down—if it went down at all—while keeping an eye out for the escaped inmate.

It was evening and the day had a cooling, gloaming, coming-to-rest quality. Subtle, desaturated, still.

Long past the time when their strained patience became hostile impatience, the guys who had already spent most of their afternoon on the river running rescue drills in hard rain helped me look for what increasingly seemed to be something that wasn't there.

Eventually, we gave up—mostly because they insisted— and I caught a ride back over to the scene of the escape in full dark. Numerous deputies and COs, joined now by the K-9 unit, were still searching the area lit by the generator-powered light tower, but the escaped inmate was proving to be as elusive as my phantom plane.

When Dad dropped me at my trailer well after midnight, I was wet, tired, and hungry. I had totaled my truck, failed to prevent an escape, and wasted a lot of time. As the fatigue and frustration set in, I felt angry and depressed, and, as usual, I was unable to find any solace in sleep.

Chapter Seven

"**I** think we've got a serial rapist here," DeLisa Lopez said.

"Actually," I said, "we've got several."

It was the next morning and I was tired, on edge. We were sitting in my office in the chapel of Potter Correctional Institution, drinking coffee from paper cups.

She frowned at me. "I mean one active now. And he's not just raping other inmates."

Though most people on the outside seem to think that brutal rape is just a part of the prison experience, in actuality it doesn't happen nearly as much as they think. There's sex inside, and some of it is coercive, but very little of it is rape in the most violent sense of the word. Inmates are watched very closely. For two of them to have sex, it has to happen so quickly and so carefully, they both have to work together to find just the right place and time. The exception to this, of course, is when there is a lapse in security, when routine and complacency make an officer sloppy or careless, but for the most part sex in prison is in some sense consensual.

That's not to say that rape doesn't still happen or that when it does it isn't violent and brutal and horrible, just that it isn't as much a part of prison as popular culture would have you believe.

"You?" I asked, alarm in my voice.

She shook her head. "Just men," she said. "Inmates, officers, support staff, but just men."

"How do you know?"

"I keep hearing the same story over and over," she said.

Nearly all day every day, Lisa sat and listened to and counseled with the inmates of PCI. Many would try to manipulate her for various reasons, but if she was hearing the same story over and over from different men, there may be something to it.

DeLisa Lopez, the dark, nearly beautiful Hispanic woman from South Florida, was a relatively new psych specialist at PCI. As usual, she made me think of heat, her sensualness more suited for a sweltering South Beach club than a North Florida prison.

A bad relationship had caused her to migrate to the Panhandle. I wasn't sure what was making her stay.

"They're not reporting it because of how humiliating it is for them," she said, "but many of them have confided in me."

"What're they saying?" I asked.

She hesitated. "If it gets out that it came from me . . ."

"It won't."

She nodded. "Somehow," she said, "he's making them rape themselves."

I thought about it, my mind reeling. No wonder they weren't reporting it. This went beyond the usual violation and humiliation of rape into a whole new form of degradation.

"Can you elaborate?" I asked.

"Not really," she said. "As you can imagine, they're not very specific, but the thing they have in common is that he's forcing them to sodomize themselves."

"You think any of them would be willing to talk to me?"

"NO," she said, raising her voice. "Absolutely not. If they ever found out I told anyone about it, my efficacy is over."

"It's not a lot to go on," I said.

"It's all I have," she said. "All I can say."

"Why tell me at all then?" I asked.

"The way you solved Justin Menge's murder," she said.

"Not just your investigative skills. Your discretion."

While investigating the murder of Justin Menge last year, I discovered that Lisa had been having an affair with one of the suspects. An inmate. She assured me it was over and that it would never happen again, so I didn't report her like I was supposed to. It was a judgment call. One I based on intuition and experience. One I had questioned several times since.

"I'm not just talking about the way you handled my stupidity," she said. "This is going to require a great deal of sensitivity."

I nodded and we fell silent a moment.

The morning light spilling into my office caused Lisa's bronze skin to shimmer, magnified her copper-colored highlights, and dappled the dark carpet with the distinctive design of razor wire.

"Will you find out who's doing it and stop him?"

"With no suspects, no witnesses I can talk to, and nothing to go on?" I said. "Don't see why I can't have it cleared up by lunchtime."

"I better get back to my office," she said. "The new warden's out to get me."

"Everybody thinks that."

"Doesn't mean it's not true," she said.

"What's not true?" Bat Matson, the new warden said, walking into my office without knocking.

Chapter Eight

Lisa tried to speak, but nothing came out.

"A lot of things," I said.

"I know you two are probably discussing an inmate you're both working with," Matson said, "but I really need to talk to the chaplain."

"I was just about to leave," Lisa said. "We were finished."

"Well, then," he said, "my timing is even better than I thought."

Lisa left and Matson took her seat across the desk from me.

Before coming to PCI a little less than a month ago, Bat Matson was the warden of the Louisiana State Penitentiary at Angola, the largest maximum security prison in the country. Known as the Farm, Angola was named after the home of African slaves who used to work its plantation. The site of a prison since the end of the Civil War, Angola's 18,000 acres houses over 5,000 men, three-quarters of whom are black, 85 percent of whom will die within its fences.

Matson had been brought to PCI by the new secretary of the department who the governor had recruited from Texas as part of his crackdown on crime platform. He was a fleshy man in his early sixties with prominent jowls and thick gray hair swooped to the side. He had the reputation of being tough, straight shooting, and very religious.

He was just one of many changes taking place at PCI,

including the relocation of death row into a newly constructed facility that housed both the row and the chair.

"Sorry I haven't gotten by here sooner, Chaplain," he said. "I've been tryin' to meet with all the department heads individually but it's taken longer than I would have liked."

"No problem," I said, not sure what kind of response he was looking for.

"I want you to know that the chapel program is very important to me," he said. "Every man here could benefit from a good dose of old-time religion."

Uh oh. I was the last chaplain who could give them that.

"I know you've been without a staff chaplain since you've been here," he said, "and that's one of the first things I'm gonna take care of. I can promise you that. I'm sure as soon as we get you some help in here a lot of the things that have gone undone will get squared away right away."

I wondered what he was talking about, but was afraid to ask. I often felt guilty for spending as much time as I did investigating, but never felt derelict in my duties as pastor of my parish.

"I've got big plans for PCI," he said.

He wasn't the only one. With a full-size institution, an annex, and two work camps, PCI was already the largest prison in the state, but having death row here would change everything in ways none of us could begin to imagine.

"Things are going to be very different," he said. "I'm a warden that backs up his staff, but I expect them to back me up as well—especially my department heads. All the changes will take some getting used to, but I expect it. I expect it or I expect your resignation."

He paused for a moment, his eyes narrowing as he considered me.

I didn't say anything.

"I'm telling that to everybody," he said, "not just you. What I will say to you is that I expect my chaplain to be a chaplain—nothing else. I understand your dad's the current sheriff, that you were a cop in Atlanta, and that you sometimes help the institutional investigator. I've met him and I can see why. But he's about to go back to coaching, and his replacement, a real investigator, won't need any help from the chaplain to do his job. You got any questions for me?"

"They found the inmate that escaped yet?"

He shook his head, then frowned, and looked at me the way you would a stubborn child you pity for how hard he makes life for himself.

"You see?" he said. "That's the kind of thing I'm talking about right there. You shouldn't be worrying about the convict that escaped—until you visit him in the infirmary or perform his funeral."

"Is he as likely to get killed as he is captured?" I asked.

"Depends on him. But between you and me—and the inmate population—I ain't afraid to kill a convict."

He stood up and looked down at me, his jowls more noticeable now.

"There's a new sheriff in town," he said. "Things are gonna be different. You'll probably have to visit more inmates in the infirmary, but I guarantee you'll visit less officers in the hospital."

He walked over to the door.

"Your new staff chaplain should be here by the end of the week," he said.

I was shocked. A position had to be advertised for at least two weeks and a committee that included the new employee's supervisor—in this case me—had to conduct interviews and make a recommendation to the warden who, if he approved it, then forwarded it to regional office.

"We haven't even advertised it yet," I said.

"Don't need to. It's already filled. I'm bringing in my favorite chaplain from the Farm. He's got a lot of experience. He's very devout. Just what we need around here."

"But—" I began.

"It's a done deal, Chaplain," he said. "Approved by the secretary."

I thought about it, my frustration rising at the absurdity and futility of the situation.

"Why would he take a demotion to come here?" I asked, figuring I already knew the answer.

He smiled and winked at me.

It was obvious. If the new warden had anything to say about it, and he did, his favorite chaplain from the Farm would be moving up into my position in no time at all.

"You have a blessed day, Chaplain Jordan," he said. "Get out there and do some good."

Chapter Nine

Michael Jensen, the inmate who had escaped, was a white man in his early forties with darkening blond hair, clear, kind blue eyes, and a dark complexion. He was probably somewhere between fifty and a hundred pounds overweight, but he carried it well.

According to his file, he had never had a single discipline referral. He was a model inmate with good adjustment serving the last few weeks of a two-year sentence for a minor drug charge.

His classification officer was as surprised as anyone that he ran.

"Of all the inmates I ever worked with," Ralph Jones, the thin, constantly moving African-American classification officer said, "Jensen would be the very last I'd ever expect to run. Dead last."

Having come from the work camp to meet with the warden, inspector, and classification supervisor about the case, Ralph had stopped in Classification to speak to a few of his friends. When I found him in the hallway and asked about Michael Jensen, he looked around nervously, grabbed my arm, and led me into an empty office.

"The new warden told me not to talk to you," he said, his small eyes wide behind his tinted glasses.

"I won't tell him."

We were standing in the empty office, the only light coming in from the window. Unable to be still, he shifted his weight often, jingling the change in his pockets and tapping his leg with the rolled-up papers in his hand.

"You think of any reason he'd run?" I asked.

He shook his head.

"Nothing's happened in the past few days? Problems with other inmates or staff?"

Ralph had the annoying habit of nodding too vigorously and making little noises while you talked. This gave two impressions—that he wasn't really listening, and that he was anxious for you to finish so he could say something he thought was more important.

"Not a thing," he said. "If I'd had any concerns I would have reported them to security."

"I know that," I said, trying to sound as reassuring as possible. "I know you're good at your job. I'm not looking for someone to blame. I'm just trying to understand why a model inmate with a few weeks left wanted to escape. That's all."

"Nothing happened that I know of," he said.

"He get any bad news from home?" I asked.

"Not that I know of."

"Who's he got at home?"

Ordinarily I wouldn't expect him to know, but I was sure he had spent a lot of time with Michael Jensen's file in the last several hours.

"Ex-wife, two kids, sister, mom," he said.

Long hall, tile floors, and cinder block walls, Classification was hard surfaces and empty spaces, and our voices echoed in the office the way those in the hallway beyond the door did.

"Where do they live?"

"All in Apalach," he said.

"You think that's where he's headed?"

His eyes narrowed behind his tinted glasses and he

nodded slowly. It seemed an attempt to look thoughtful, but came off as contrived. "They always go home," he said, pausing a moment before adding, "eventually."

"But why?" I said. "What happened? What was so bad, so urgent, that it couldn't wait a few weeks?"

He rubbed his chin, frowning and shaking his head as he thought about it. "We may never know. He may not even know."

"He was on his way back to the work camp from being here to see Medical," I said.

He nodded.

"What for?"

He shrugged. "You'd have to ask them about that."

Chapter Ten

Terry Little's nurse uniform was faded and slightly wrinkled. It fit loosely in a failed attempt to mask fat. It along with her melted-ice-cream figure gave her the shape of a snowman. She had short, odd-colored bottle-blond hair, cut in a dated style. She had prescription glasses designed to darken in the sun and lighten inside, but always seemed stuck in a caramel-colored in-between position.

We were standing at the back side of the medical building in the small designated smoking area where she was nervously puffing on a long skinny cigarette. When she wasn't puffing, which wasn't often, she scratched the polish off her fingernails. Always fidgety, her encounter with the new warden and her supervisor about Michael Jensen's visit yesterday had kicked her nervous shakes into hyperactivity.

When I was a kid and she was a teenager, Terry used to babysit for me, Jake, and Nancy, and though we weren't close and had never been, we shared the connection of growing up together, which created a certain trust, an assurance born of familiarity. If she knew something about Jensen she would tell me.

"Heard you got some quality time with the new warden," I said.

"What an asshole," she said, blowing smoke out forcefully, then picking a small piece of tobacco from her tongue.

"Did he tell you not to talk to me?"

She nodded, cutting her eyes toward me momentarily. "Said not to talk to anyone. Then he singled you out."

I nodded.

"So whatta you wanna know?"

I smiled. "Thanks. How did he seem?"

"Like an arrogant asshole," she said. "Like a—"

"Not Matson," I said. "Jensen."

"Oh," she said, her face flushing. "Sorry. He was more quiet than usual."

"You'd treated him before?"

"Lots of times," she said. "He was diabetic."

"That why he was here this time?"

She nodded.

The early afternoon sun was high in a cloudless sky. And blindingly bright. The light glinting off of the chain link and razor wire above us reflected up off the white concrete pad beneath us. But far worse than the bright light was the humid heat. It bore down on us with an incredible intensity, a heat that made people lethargic, ill, even homicidal.

If she hadn't needed a cigarette and I didn't need to get information from her in secrecy, I wouldn't be out here. I'd be in the chapel, and like many of the inmates cooling off there right now, it would not be for spiritual reasons.

"He was here while we changed his medication," she said.

"How long?" I asked.

"A couple of days for observation after we changed it," she said. "Less than a week."

So whatever happened to make him do what he did, probably happened here.

"He seemed despondent," she said. "Depressed. And angry. He was very upset about something. Maybe I just think that because of what happened, but I don't really think so."

I thought about what she was saying.

"I should've done more for him," she said. "Tried to find out what was really going on with him. He was one of the best inmates I've ever worked with. I hate that this happened."

"Any ideas what was bothering him?"

She frowned, twisting her round face and raising her eyebrows. "I could be wrong," she said. "I hope I am. I really do. But I've worked with a lot of them over the years, and I know the signs. I can usually tell when they walk in the door. Why didn't I say something, do more?"

"About what?" I asked.

She sighed heavily. "I think he had been raped."

Chapter Eleven

I lived alone in an antiquated mobile home near the Apalachicola River in The Prairie Palm II—phase two of a failed trailer park community consisting of a single resident.

When I first moved back to Pottersville from Atlanta, this was all I could find or afford. I had planned to stay here only temporarily, but should have taken one look at The Prairie Palm II and known what happens to plans around here.

The truth was, I found this Spartan existence liberating, this isolated tin box on the outskirts of a tiny backwoods town appropriate for the marginal life I was living.

This felt like a choice to me, not something foisted on me.

Unable to sleep much at night, I occasionally came home from work, laid down on my uncomfortable couch, and attempted to read until I drifted off, telling myself all I needed was about ten good minutes to take the ache out of my head and the burn from behind my eyes. This rarely worked—it wasn't just at night that I had trouble sleeping—but that didn't stop me from continuing to try it.

I was rereading Thomas Moore's book *Dark Nights of the Soul*, attempting to feel sleepy, when I heard someone pull up outside.

I was reading the book again not only because I loved Moore's insight, honesty, and low soulish spirituality, but because I believed myself to be experiencing an extended dark night of the soul. After years of an intensely intimate, nearly mystical spiritual life, I felt dead inside. All my attempts to regain what I once had falling far short, I felt comforted by Moore's encouragement to embrace the darkness and emptiness, allowing this depleting experience to have its way with me, trusting that its difficult gifts were necessary for my evolving humanity.

Of course it was possible that I was just depressed.

I slipped the tattered envelope I was using for a bookmark between the pages, closed the book, replaced it on my TBR pile on the floor, and pushed myself up off the couch.

Sliding the thin, wrinkled blind slightly to the side, I squinted in the bright light in an attempt to identify my visitor.

When I saw the old burgundy Dodge pickup, I knew who it was. The truck belonged to Rudy, the owner of the local diner named after him. But it wasn't Rudy, it was his teenage daughter Carla who had come calling.

Carla and I spent a lot of time together at night in Rudy's Diner where she worked and I didn't sleep. She had natural blond hair and large green eyes and the permanent sadness of a motherless child.

As I opened the dented and leaning door, she was out of the truck and approaching the trailer. She had almost reached it when an emaciated hunting dog dove out of the back of the truck, landed face first on the ground, jumped up, and started barking and running around wildly.

She shook her head and frowned in frustration. "I wanted to talk you into taking him before you saw him."

"I can see why."

Not only was he loud, wild, and malnourished, but he was missing hair in spots and had red patches on his ears and legs.

Moving about frantically, he would occasionally dash toward us, always stopping short, yelp loudly, then run back.

She turned toward him, leaned forward, and began to call him. "Walker. Walker. Here Walker. Come here boy."

Like Walker, Carla was much thinner than she should be, and I worried that she might be anorexic. She had a new boyfriend, and lately she had been far more withdrawn, far less confiding, far more self-conscious.

I ducked back into the trailer and grabbed some sandwich meat from the refrigerator. When I joined Carla in the yard I knelt down on the ground and held out the meat. Walker barked at me but refused to come close enough to take the meat from my outstretched hand. I broke off a little piece of the meat the threw it to him. He jerked back from the meat and ran away a few steps before coming back and inhaling it.

"He's been getting into the garbage behind the diner," she said. "I'm afraid Rudy's gonna shoot him."

"He'd have to have good aim," I said.

She laughed.

I held out the meat again and though he didn't want to come close to me his hunger got the better of him and he slowly and warily walked over. As he ate the meat from one hand, I slowly raised my other one to pet him. He cowered and crouched down, wetting the ground beneath him as he did.

"It's okay," I said, in that silly voice humans use to talk to animals and babies. "I'm not gonna hurt you."

Walker was mostly white with two large black spots on his back and sides and brown around his face and ears. He had short hair, a long narrow tail, brandy-brown eyes, and was of indeterminate breed.

"Obviously he was abused before he was abandoned," she said. "Son of a bitch. Most rednecks are better to their hunting dogs than their kids. Not this bastard."

"You got a particular bastard in mind?" I asked.

She shook her head. "Plenty enough around."

"He'll probably come looking for him when hunting season starts," I said.

"But he won't recognize him all filled out and healthy, with his shiny new coat and collar that says 'Walker Jordan.'"

I laughed.

"Besides," she said, "you get him fixed he won't want him."

"You know I may have a few plans of my own between now and hunting season," I said.

"What?" she said. "Reading a bunch of books? Hanging out at the diner at night? Dreaming about Anna? What?"

"That all you think I do?"

"I guess occasionally you teach somebody something about God or solve a murder, but those things don't take up enough of your time. You need a hobby."

"So really when you think about it," I said, "you're doing me a favor."

"It's what I do," she said. "Spread sunshine. Give help to the hopeless. Shit like that."

Finished with the meat, Walker stuck out his right paw to me and I took it. When I let go, he darted away, circling us and barking.

As I stood, I could see Merrill pulling up on the other side of Rudy's truck, his new black BMW shining in the sun the way his skin did when he got out.

Walker ran toward him barking but stopped long before he reached him and ran back, then repeated the same process several times as Merrill walked over to us.

"He's not barking at you because you're black," I said.

"That's a relief," he said. "Thought I's gonna have to cap his ass."

When Walker risked coming over to us again, he stood on his back legs and extended his right paw again, exposing his erect penis and the urine it was squirting.

"Damn," Merrill said.

"He's had a hard life," Carla said.

"So have I," Merrill said. "But you don't see me flashing

my credentials around and pissin' on everybody."

I laughed. "Everybody deals with trauma in their own way."

"Speaking of which," Carla said, "I better get Dad's truck back before he realizes it's gone."

She started moving toward the truck slowly, head down, shoulders hunched, as if expecting to be called back.

"I'm gonna need some help with the mutt," I said. "Being a single parent and all."

She smiled, and it was the happiest I had seen her in quite a while. "I'm sure we can work out a visitation schedule without a judge."

"I hope so, Carla, I really do," I said. "I just want what's best for Walker."

"That's what we both want, John. We'll always put him first."

She got in the truck and drove away, Merrill, Walker, and I staring after her, though Merrill and I didn't run around and bark.

"Convict still in the wind?" he asked.

I nodded.

He turned and looked toward the river winding around the back of the property. Smiling to himself, he looked back at Walker as the dog darted nervously around wetting himself. "Least now he float down the river and roll up in here on you, you got protection."

I smiled.

"We go get a steak," he said, "you think he'll be here when we get back?"

I looked over at his car. "We could take him."

"Out back and drown him in the river," he said, laughing. "Shee-it."

"Don't listen to Uncle Merrill," I said to Walker, who barked back, as if on cue.

He shook his head. "See? Had that mutt two minutes

and already sounding like all those other fools."

"I was being—"

Before I could finish, the phone rang. I stepped into the trailer to get it. Walker ran up the wobbly wooden steps behind me, but didn't come in, just stood there lifting his paw and barking.

When I answered, Dad said, "Can you get a ride down to the end of the road?"

"Yeah," I said. "Merrill's here."

"You might not want to bring him," he said.

"Why's that?"

"Because," he said, "there's been a lynching."

Chapter Twelve

In the South lynching has a legacy only second to slavery. It is as charged a way to die as there is, and whoever had used it as a method for murder had to know that.

I had no way of knowing what the crime scene Merrill and I were racing toward held, but a typical lynching was the hanging of a supposed criminal by outraged citizens taking justice in their own hands.

Vigilante justice was one thing. Lynching was something else entirely.

Xenophobia taken to its ultimate end, lynching was the extension of the holocaust of slavery, the terrorizing and brutalizing of a small minority by a mob mad with fear and paranoia.

Merrill Monroe and I had been friends for what seemed like our whole lives. He was the best friend I had ever had. He was far closer to me than my own family. He knew me better than anyone else on the planet. Perhaps the reverse was just as true, but that didn't mean I knew him very well. As close as we were, I had never gotten past the last layer that made his detachment and self-containment possible.

Since I had told him what Dad had said, he had driven in silence, and it seemed as if a world had opened up between us.

"You okay?" I asked.

He didn't say anything.

I had always respected his need for a certain amount

of distance—I understood it, needed it too—and had never attempted to press him very far beyond where he seemed comfortable.

"We don't even know what we're gonna find," I said.

"Oh I know what we'a find," he said. "'Nother nigger strung up."

Often playfully using the word *nigga*, Merrill reserved *nigger* for the rarest of occasions.

"Neck stretched, eyes bulging," he continued. "You know goddamn well what we'll find. Sheriff wouldn't've said not to bring me if it was something else."

He was racing down the twisting road that led across the dam and dead-ended at the river, and as he talked he sped up even more.

I had seen him joke his way through some of the most difficult and traumatic situations imaginable, often coping with a nearly preternatural coolness. I could count on one hand the number of times I had seen him like this.

"Anything I can do?" I asked.

"Nothin' nobody can do," he said. "Nothing changes. Nobody—fuck it. It's just one more dead nigger."

We rode the rest of the way in silence and when we reached the end of the road he surprised me by not parking but pulling up to drop me off.

All around us, deputies, game wardens, search and rescue, EMTs, and crime scene techs from FDLE rushed around, strobed by the flashing lights from their vehicles.

I could sense their urgency, feel the pull of the excitement and energy, but I didn't move.

We sat there a long moment, neither of us saying anything. After a while, he nodded. I looked over at him. When he looked back at me, I nodded, then got out.

Remaining behind at the crime scene, Dad sent Jake to the landing to pick me up. When I stepped into the boat and saw how visibly shaken Jake was, I realized part of the reason Dad sent him was to get him away.

"How bad is it?" I asked.

He shook his head. "It's the worst thing I've ever . . ."

Since joining search and rescue, Jake had lost some weight and gotten some color, and he more closely resembled the handsome high school quarterback he had been a decade ago. His green deputy's uniform no longer strained to hold in his gut and his face had regained some of its angularity.

"Can you tell me about it?" I asked.

"Be better if you see it. It's just a few minutes away."

Along the banks of the river, campers and permanent residents had come out of their cabins, trailers, and campers and were standing on their docks straining to see what was happening.

"Where're we going?" I asked.

"Close to where we were yesterday. Not far from where the inmate escaped."

"It's not him, is it?" I asked.

He shrugged. "Could be."

"Whatta you mean could be? Did you look at him or not?"

"The victim?" he asked. "Hell, I thought you meant the perpetrator. He ain't the victim. The victim's black."

"Got an ID on him yet?"

"Not when I left. Hard to tell just by looking at him. He's in bad shape."

We were in a different, smaller search and rescue boat that bounced over the wakes of the larger boats in the olive-green waters. The sun was low in the sky, just barely above the tree tops to the west, its light and heat less relentless now, and as we rounded the last bend and I could see the other emergency

services boats tied to trees along the bank, I wondered how long
we had until it would be too dark to see beneath the thick trees.

Jake pulled up beside one the game warden's boats, cut
the engine, and I jumped out onto the damp sand with the bow
line. The wake from our boat created large ripples that rolled in
and receded like waves, slapping at the banks, tree bases, and the
hulls of the boats. After securing the boat to the exposed roots
of a cypress tree that would be under water if the river was
higher, I looked over at Jake.

"I'm gonna wait here a minute," he said.

I nodded. "You okay?"

"Will be."

I hesitated a moment.

"I'll be there in a minute," he said. "Go on. I'm fine."

I nodded, then turned, climbed the bank, ducked
beneath the crime scene tape strung around the trees, and
walked toward the horror waiting for me in the woods beyond.

It was like so many old photographs I had seen—gray, lifeless
body, elongated, stretched neck, unnaturally up-tilted head.

A rope had been thrown over a large oak limb, then
pulled around the trunk of the tree for leverage. Its noose held
a naked black man high above the ground, his feet and hands
bound, the ashen skin of his swollen body filled with cuts and
gashes.

It was one of the most horrific things I had ever seen.

It wasn't just the death but the degradation. Not only
what had been done to the body but the way it was displayed.
His nakedness in particular, the indecency of his indignity.
The raw, exposed, unflattering way his soft belly and breasts
hung, the way his long, hard, yellowish toenails protruded from
his wide, flat feet, and most of all the way his flaccid phallus
dangled lifelessly for all beneath him to see.

Disquieting. Unsettling. Disturbing. Truly traumatizing.

In the near silence the shocking scene elicited, the only sounds beside whispers were those of the stretching rope straining against the tree and the torpid, rhythmic creaking of the branch as a breeze slowly swung the body side to side.

When Dad saw me he walked over.

"Can you believe this?"

I shook my head. "It's as shocking as it's meant to be."

We were standing alone inside the wide circle of deputies, search and rescue, EMTs, and game wardens.

"We're waiting on FDLE to process the scene," he said. "They're heading over now from the landing."

"Any idea who he is?" I asked.

He shook his head. "No one here recognizes him so far."

"You find his clothes?" I asked.

"Nothing," he said. "No clothes, no shoes, no boat, no nothing."

The body was hanging from a large oak tree in the midst of a hardwood hammock, surrounded by a thick canopy of magnolia, pine, oak, and cypress trees, beneath which grew a dense web of weeds, ferns, grass, and bamboo. Scattered all around were fallen trees, limbs, and leaves, very little light penetrating the full August foliage.

"Who found him?" I asked.

"COs from the prison looking for the escaped inmate."

"You find anything to indicate it might have been a mob or the Klan?"

He shook his head. "No markings or symbols on the ground or trees. And not a single footprint."

I looked past the body at the seemingly impenetrable woods beyond.

"How far to the nearest road?" I asked.

"A few miles," he said, following my gaze. "No way he brought him through there."

"Unless the killer didn't bring him. They could have

walked together."

He shrugged. "Maybe," he said, "but it's more likely they came by boat."

I nodded. "Why do it in such an isolated area?" I said. "He killed him in a way that is meant to be seen—to shock and horrify."

He looked to be thinking about it, then said, "That's what I want you to figure out."

FDLE arrived and began to process the scene. As they took pictures and set up their equipment, Dad gathered all the local law enforcement together.

"What we've got here is a murder," he said, "and that's what we need to call it. This investigation will require far more sensitivity than most."

As Dad spoke, I looked around the group of mostly men listening to him. Between the deputies, the search and rescue team, and the correctional officers, there were three men present who were running for sheriff. Standing next to Todd, Shane, Sandy, and Jake who had just joined us, Fred Goodwin looked bored with what Dad was saying and distracted by the FDLE techs behind him.

"I realize what this looks like," Dad was saying, "but for now this is just a murder. Until we're absolutely certain, I don't want to hear anything about race or mobs or lynching. Understand?"

I looked to see the reaction of the handful of African-Americans mixed in among all the white faces. There wasn't one—beyond drawn faces, hollow eyes, and clenched jaws.

"And one more thing," he said. "I realize this is an election year and some of you here want my job. That's fine. If you win and get it, I'll shake your hand and help you in any way I can. You can count on that. But until that happens, I'm still the sheriff and I'm in charge. Understand?"

Only a few within the crowd nodded or gave any indication they were even listening.

"We're all professional law enforcement officers first," he said. "You clear everything through me. You bring everything to me—no matter how small it may seem. And I better not hear of anyone trying to use this or any other case for political purposes. This isn't political. This is life. This is death. The man hanging up there in that tree is someone's son, maybe someone's husband or father. He deserves the best we can give him, not what we can get from him."

Fred Goodwin began clapping slowly. "Well said, Sheriff," he said. "Well said. Now let's all work together to catch the son of a bitch who did this, and this time let's share the credit for solving the case when we're done."

Chapter Thirteen

"**C**ould your inmate have done this?" Rachel Mills asked.

I looked over at the body. Having processed the scene, FDLE was now lowering it and I could see it better.

"My inmate?"

"The one you let escape," she said with a smile.

It was dark now. Large halogen lights powered by generators partially illuminated the crime scene, but next to me much of Rachel's short frame, pale skin, straight blond hair, and light blue eyes were in shadow.

"From the little I've learned about him so far I'd say no."

An aggressive FDLE agent, who was now a friend, Rachel had once investigated me because of allegations made by the wife of an inmate—allegations she was sure were true. It's how we met. In this case, Rachel would serve as FDLE's lead investigator and liaison to the sheriff's department.

Having sent most of the other law enforcement agencies home, Dad had only a few deputies posted around the perimeter of the crime scene, and he, Fred Goodwin, Jake, and Robert Pridgeon stood together opposite Rachel and me on the other side of the body.

As the sheriff's department's lead homicide detective, Fred Goodwin would head the investigation, and as the senior game warden, Robert Pridgeon would represent the game and freshwater fish commission on the makeshift task force.

"If not him, who?" Rachel asked.

I shrugged.

"Of course, where would he get the rope?" she said.

"A camp. Houseboat. May belong to this guy."

"So you think it's possible?" she asked.

I nodded. "No one expected him to escape."

"And if it's not him?"

"Somebody with a boat," I said.

"That's half the population around here," she said.

We were quiet for a moment.

Eventually she said, "Could be the brother or father of the white girl he was dating."

She was right. It could be.

FDLE had lowered the body so that the feet were just above the ground and were now studying and photographing it. As bad as the body had looked hanging high above the ground, it looked even worse now. In addition to the bloodless cuts and gashes in the gray and bloated skin around the head and chest, everything was swollen to grotesque proportions.

"I hate to be the one to point this out," she said, "but shouldn't his hands be covering his genitals?"

I took a closer look at the body.

She was right. His bound hands would have covered most of his swollen genitals if they had been allowed to fall naturally. Instead, the killer had tied a length of rope around his neck to the one binding his hands so that they rested higher on his body than they normally would.

"You're right," I said.

"Think it's intentional?" she asked.

I nodded.

We were quiet for another moment, each of us looking at the atrocity inflicted on this man.

"Any Klan around here?" she asked.

"Not that I know of, but I wouldn't exactly be on their

mailing list."

She laughed.

"There may not be an organized Klan," I said, "but there's plenty of Klanishness."

"Klanishness?" she said.

I nodded.

It was difficult to tell from here, but it appeared that the front of the victim's body held the faint purplish tint of fixed lividity. The body had suffered so much trauma and was so swollen, we might not ever know for sure.

"You dating anybody?" she asked without looking at me.

I shook my head. "Not at the moment."

"You still hung up on what's-her-name? The lawyer's wife?"

"How'd you know about that?"

"FDLE bitches," she said. "Are you?"

"Trying not to be," I said. "But so far they haven't come out with a patch for that."

"If you want to go out sometime," she said, "just for fun or some amazing sex . . . let me know."

"How amazing?" I asked.

She laughed.

As inappropriate as it was, I was grateful for the diversion. I really needed it at the moment and suspected she did too.

"You often ask guys out at crime scenes?"

"Not just guys," she said. "And if I didn't I'd never get laid. It's sort of like being an actor on location."

I nodded. "So what're you doing Friday night?"

She looked up at me. "Really?"

"You like Cajun food?"

She nodded. "Love it."

Dad walked over to us.

"How long will it take you to solve this thing little lady?" he said to Rachel.

"Hoping to have it wrapped up by Friday," she said. "Got plans Friday night."

He looked at me. "Can you believe this?"

I shook my head.

"I don't want this to be my last case," he said.

"It won't be," Rachel said. "We'll clear this in no time and give you all the credit. You'll win by a landslide."

"You sure?" he asked.

"Positive," she said, "and I'm never wrong."

He gave her an incredulous look. "Aren't you the one who thought John was guilty of assaulting and raping that inmate's wife?"

Chapter Fourteen

"**Y**ou think it was racially motivated?" Anna asked.

I shrugged. "Hard not to."

She nodded.

"Can't imagine he'd've been hanging from a tree if he were white," I added.

Off for the past few days, Anna had stopped by the chapel on her first day back to find me in the sanctuary unsuccessfully attempting to meditate.

The sanctuary was dim, its only illumination the morning sunlight streaming in the exterior door on the side and the few candles I had lit on the altar.

Finding it far easier to deal with my feelings for her when I didn't see her, Anna and I hadn't spent nearly as much time together lately as we had in the past. I hadn't avoided her exactly, but I hadn't sought her out like I normally did either.

"I still can't believe it," she said. "It's probably set race relations back fifty years around here."

"And they were already at least that far back to begin with," I said.

"What did Merrill say?" she asked.

"It bothered him more than anything I've seen in a long time—just the idea of it. He didn't even go to the scene. Didn't even see it and—"

"And now everybody has," she said.

Several area papers had run a color photo from the crime scene on the front page above the fold that showed in detail the horror of what had happened.

"It would've been bad enough if everyone just heard about it," she said, "but to actually see a picture . . ."

I nodded.

"How'd they get it?" she asked.

"My guess?" I said. "Someone running against Dad."

She shook her head.

It could have just been the flicker of the candlelight or the dimness of the room, but Anna looked pale, her eyes hollow, large dark circles beneath them.

"Do you think things will ever get better?" she asked.

I nodded. "Our generation is far less racist than our parents'. From what I've seen of Carla and her friends, their's is better than ours. But there's still so much beneath the surface. We've got a hell of a long way to go. And there will always be ignorant, hateful holdouts."

She shook her head. "Some people are so militant about it. I wonder if it'll ever get better."

"The militant racists are like religious fundamentalists," I said. "They're reacting to the change they see. It scares them. We'll always have them, but they're in the minority—which is why they're so desperate."

"What's going on?" she asked. "You're usually not this optimistic."

I smiled.

I always felt more optimistic when I was with Anna, as if the world that was meant to be was still possible.

"I'm not sure what it is," I said, "but I feel suddenly inspired."

"Must be your morning prayers."

I looked at her and smiled again, our eyes locking for a long moment.

"I've missed you," she said.

Tears formed in her eyes and she attempted to blink them back. When they crested, she wiped at the corners of her eyes with her fingertips.

"What is it?" I asked.

She started to say something, but stopped.

"Are you okay?"

She stood. "I've got to go."

"Anna."

"I'm sorry," she said. "I'm fine. I'm just being silly. Really. I'll talk to you later."

I stood and moved toward her. When I reached out for her, she shook her head and backed away.

"I'm okay," she said, her voice stronger, her tears and sniffles stopping suddenly.

The back doors of the chapel opened and I turned to see the warden walk in with who could only be my new staff chaplain.

He had the permed hair, pinched look that said Pentecostal preacher. At least twenty years my senior, he had large, ovalish glasses, a lot of loose skin, a couple of extra chins, and a gut that tumbled down over his belt.

Walking out quickly, Anna passed them halfway down the center aisle.

"Mrs. Rodden," the warden said, emphasizing the fact that she was married, though Rodden wasn't her married name.

"Ms.," she said, nodding toward them, but not slowing down.

When the two men reached me, the warden said, "Every time I come in here there's a woman leaving."

"All both times," I said.

"John Jordan," he said, ignoring me, "this is Chaplain Daniel Singer, the best chaplain I've ever had the privilege of working with."

I extended my hand and Singer's shot out to meet it

aggressively. Though his grip was tight, his pumps violent, his hands were soft and clammy, which sabotaged the statement he was trying to make.

"It's nice to meet you," I said. "Welcome."

"Praise God, brother, it's good to here," he said.

"I know you two have a lot to talk about," the warden said, "but I need to see Chaplain Jordan for a moment. Dan, why don't you take a look around the chapel?"

"Sounds good," Singer said, and moved off in the direction of the kitchen in the back.

Before he was out of earshot, the warden said, "Just what the hell're you doing?"

I immediately straightened and stiffened, my entire being growing wary and defensive.

"You know how it looks for you to be in here with a married woman with all the lights off?"

"All depends on who's looking," I said.

He started to say something, but stopped, pursed his lips tightly, frowned, and shook his head. "The reason I wanted to talk to you is I keep hearing you're still playing detective even though I told you not to do anything but be the best damn chaplain you can be."

I didn't say anything.

This seemed to make him even more angry.

"Consider this your final warning," he said. "If I find out that you're continuing to investigate instead of preach, you'll be able to be a full-time investigator somewhere else."

Hovering near the back of the sanctuary, Singer seemed to sense that it was time for him to rejoin us. When he did, the warden patted him on the back and said, "I can't tell you how good it is to have you here." Turning to me, he said, "Chaplain, there's a lot you can learn from this man. I hope you'll take advantage of this opportunity."

Looking down in what seemed to me to be false humility, Singer said, "Well, I'm just a humble servant of the Lord, but

I am still on fire just as much after all these years. I've got a burden for souls, brother. A burden for souls. We might not keep these men out of prison, but by God we've got to keep them out of hell."

Speaking of hell. I had just been dropped into it.

I couldn't believe what was happening. This was even worse than I had imagined it could be.

I shook my head, laughed to myself, and said, "Should I go ahead and start cleaning out my desk?"

Chapter Fifteen

As usual, the kitchen of PCI was hot and humid, its damp air thick with the unappetizing smells of processed food, old grease, sweat, sour body odor, and commercial insecticide. Perhaps because of its association with food, I found it to be the most unpleasant place on the compound. It wasn't a place I frequented often, and I never stayed any longer than I absolutely had to.

I had come on this hot August afternoon to see an inmate known as Dil. Most inmates had nicknames. Few fit as well as this one. Named for the character Jaye Davidson played in *The Crying Game*, Dil was easily the prettiest, most feminine man I had ever seen.

Dil had many admirers and lovers on the compound, and I was sure one of them worked in the barber shop. Dil did not have a typical inmate buzz cut botch job. Longer than regulation, which meant her admirers weren't limited to inmates, her curly hair was cut stylishly, even lovingly, and accentuated her beauty.

I found her bent over a large pan of cinnamon rolls on an enormous industrial stainless steel table. A tub of thin white icing in one hand, a dull rubber butter knife in the other, she was busy slathering each roll with an abundance of the sugary paste.

When she saw me, her seductive, slightly sad eyes

widened and she smiled.

"Hey, Chaplain," she said in her most flirty voice. "Haven't seen you in a while. Where you been keepin' your fine self?"

"How are you Dil?"

"Be better if you give me a job in the chapel," she said.

"From what I hear they can't do without you down here."

"Same would soon be true if I worked up there, honey. And I guarantee your church attendance would go up."

I laughed. "I don't doubt that."

She was leaning over in such a way that her small backside was sticking out, and she wiggled it often as she shifted her weight from side to side.

"The lady shrink said you might stop by," she said. "I told her you could come by and see me anytime."

DeLisa Lopez had called me earlier in the afternoon and told me that Dil had information about the rapist and was willing to talk.

"I appreciate that," I said.

Beneath her wavy black hair, Dil's mocha skin was smooth and flawless. Her long lashes were coated with small amounts of mascara, her lids with a light dusting of purplish eyeshadow. Though contraband required to be confiscated if found, she always managed to have makeup. It was rumored to belong to the wife of an officer she was giving blow jobs to.

"Whatta you wanna know?" she asked, putting down the bowl of icing and tossing the knife into it.

"Do we have an active serial rapist at work around here?"

She nodded. "A real rough boy. Prolific prick too. Lots of men around here carry his mark."

"His mark?"

She tilted her head back and put her small balled-up fist

at the top of her neck below her left ear. "He holds a shank
to their neck while he does it. Always cuts 'em a little bit, but
if they squirm or squeal he cuts 'em bad. The pound's full of
punks he's done turned out."

"And they all have a scar right under their jaw line?"
She nodded.

"How do you know all this?" I asked.

"You'd be surprised what the men 'round here confide in
me," she said. "Guess I'm just easy to talk to."

"Yeah," I said, "I was just about to tell you all my
secrets."

She laughed. "Chaplain, you ain't got no secrets."

"Everybody has secrets. You should know that."

She smiled. "I was thinking maybe everybody but you."

I laughed. "They tell you anything else?"

She nodded. "Lots."

"Does he do the same thing to everybody?"

She nodded again. "He attacks them from behind, beats
them bad on their body beneath their clothes, puts a hood of
some sort around their head and a shank to their throat. He
only whispers so you don't ever really hear his voice. They say
he's all calm and shit. Tells them he gonna slit their throat and
fuck 'em while they bleed to death if they yell for help or try
to get away, but if they cooperate it'll be over soon and they'll
live. Then he pulls down their pants and makes them rape
themselves."

"How so?"

"He spits on their finger and makes them . . . you know
. . . rape themselves with it," she said. "Sometimes he makes
them insert an object of some kind. Everything that happens he
makes them do to themselves."

A painting I'd seen somewhere by Salvador Dalí drifting
up from my subconscious popped into my head and I tried to
recall the title. I couldn't quite remember, but it was something
like "Young Woman Autosodomized by Her Own..."

something maybe. I would have to remember to pull down one of the books I have of his work and look it up later.

"You know of anybody it's happened to who'll talk to me?" I asked.

"You know which cons'll talk to you," she said. "Just look for the telltale scars."

Chapter Sixteen

After leaving the kitchen, I decided to see if the inmate library had a book of Salvador Dalí's work. I was anxious to see it and didn't want to wait until I got home. On my way I ran into Merrill, who had been called in on his day off.

"What I get for answerin' my damn phone," he said, shaking his head.

We were standing near the educational building across from the laundry. All around us, inmates were moving about—a steady stream flowing to and from Medical, Psychology, the chapel, and the library. Those assigned to inside grounds were sweeping the asphalt road that ran the length of the compound and the sidewalks to either side of it, while others were kneeling around the rows of flowers in between them—pruning, weeding, and replanting.

"We operating at critical?" I asked.

Each shift had critical limits it was not allowed to operate below. When personnel dropped beneath that number, an officer who was told he was needed, could lose his job if he didn't report for duty—even if he had just completed the shift he was assigned to.

"You haven't heard? They scared there might be a riot."

"Over what?"

"The hanging nigger on the front page of the paper,"

he said. "They made sure none of today's papers got on the 'pound, but some of the inmates on the outside work crews saw one and are already sayin' they's gonna be an uprising. They called a bunch of us in to be here when the work squads come back in this evening."

"To discourage the uprising?" I said, smiling.

"Stomp the shit out of it was the word I got," he said.

Of the many officers passing us on their way down to the compound, a handful were dressed in the special uniforms of the riot squad. Todd Sears and Shane Bryant were among them. In addition to search and rescue and the riot squad, they were also both on the pistol team. Had the prison not been built in Pottersville they may very well be doing time somewhere, but as it was they were well paid to do things they loved.

As they rushed by they waved to us, Shane yelling to Merrill, "Ready to crack some skulls?"

When they had passed by, he shook his head. "They love this soldier shit. Redneck take any opportunity to beat a nigger."

I nodded but didn't say anything. Something was bothering Merrill—and it wasn't just the normal pain of being a smart, sensitive man of color living in the deep South.

"You figured out who strung him up yet?" he asked.

Though attempting to sound like his normal playful self, he wasn't quite pulling it off. I could hear it in his words and the tension in his voice.

"You okay?" I asked.

"Don't take a clerical detective to deduce I'm not, do it?"

"Well don't make me try to figure out what it is," I said. "Just tell me. What is it?"

He looked down the compound, gazing into the distance, his jaw muscles flexing beneath his dark skin. As I watched him, I realized that I had come to see him as invincible—both physically and emotionally impenetrable, and it was only on a rare occasion like this one that I was reminded otherwise.

"Everybody—including my mama—will tell you it was just a nightmare," he said, "that I just dreamed the whole thing, that I was too young, just heard about one and it bothered me so bad that I couldn't deal with it, but when I was little I saw a lynching."

"Around here?"

"In the woods behind our house," he said. "Well, really it was behind the church next door to our house. Preacher used to come from Marianna twice a month. I don't know what he did, probably spoke to some white woman while he was getting gas or something, but they beat him unconscious, put a noose around his neck, pissed on him to wake him up, then yanked him up and let him swing."

"How old were you?"

He shrugged. "Four or five. Maybe. Don't know for sure."

I shook my head. "I'm so sorry, man," I said. "Why haven't you ever said anything?"

"Wouldn't've said anything now if I hadn't been acting the damn fool."

I waited, wanting him to say more, wanting to comfort or reassure him, but unsure how.

Seeming anxious to change the subject, he said, "What do you know about the river nigger?"

"Next to nothing," I said. "No ID, no evidence, no autopsy yet."

"Why hang him way down there? You think the escaped con did it? What's his name?"

"Jensen," I said. "Don't know enough about him or why he ran yet. Can't rule him out though."

He nodded.

"Guess I better get on over to the south gate so I be ready if a riot break out," he said.

"If you want, we can try to find out who killed the preacher you saw and where they put him," I said. "What was his name?"

"Last thing I heard him called was nigger," he said. "Just another dead nigger."

Chapter Seventeen

I entered the enormous building that housed the inmate library and made my way through the dented metal shelves that held the worn paperbacks, their pages ripped and torn, their tattered covers half hanging off the bindings.

Inmates filled the comfortable, air-conditioned building the way they did the chapel on hot days like these, browsing the shelves for something they hadn't read ten times, donning headphones and listening to audiobooks, meeting with one of the inmate law clerks in the law library along the back, but mostly just prolonging their stay in the cool, quiet environment. It was one of only a few oases in the hot, humid, noisy wasteland that was PCI.

When I first became a chaplain every prison library in the state had a qualified librarian. Now many of them were overseen by non-degreed officers with little or no training. Of the officers who regularly rotated through the library, many of whom approached it as a babysitting job, the very best was Sandy Hartman.

A reader himself, Sandy was knowledgeable and helpful, quick with a recommendation or a review. I found him in the librarian's office reading a paperback without a cover.

He stood when I walked in and placed the book on the desk.

"They already read the cover off that one?" I asked.

He smiled, his face red from his time on the river the day before. "Actually this one came that way," he said. "We have a bunch of them that do."

"Really?"

"You keep a secret?" he asked. "When paperbacks don't sell, the bookstores don't ship them back like they do hardcovers. They strip the covers off and return them and throw away the actual books. I think the shipping costs more than the book is worth."

I recalled seeing the warning in front of many mass market paperbacks about coverless books.

"When I told the manager of one of the bookstores in Panama City how small our budget was out here," he continued, "she said she knew a way she could help, but if it got out she'd lose her job. I've been picking up her trash ever since."

He waited but I didn't say anything.

"I know it's wrong," he said, "but the thought of all these books being thrown away when they could do so much good here . . . It just bothered me."

I nodded.

"They found Jensen yet?" he asked.

I shook my head.

"What about your plane?"

I shook my head again. "Thanks for your help searching for it," I said. "Sorry to waste the team's time."

"You didn't. Usually not finding anything is a good thing. Hopefully it didn't go down."

I nodded. "Must not have. Somebody would have seen or heard something or reported it missing by now."

"Sorry for how the guys act," he said.

"The SAR team? I'm used to it. Hell, one of 'em's my brother."

"He's not too bad. Not compared to the others. Some of them . . . I really like to dive and I'm pretty good at it—and

I want to help, you know, make a difference, but I just can't deal with all their . . . bullshit anymore. I resigned yesterday. Anyway . . . I know you're not here to talk about any of that. How can I help you?"

"I'm looking for a book of Salvador Dali's work."

"I've got a couple. Right this way."

He led me to a large wooden bookcase inmates had built just outside his office. It had oversized shelves and held large, heavy art, architecture, and photography books.

He found three Dali books and pulled them from the shelves.

"You looking for something in particular?" he asked.

"Yeah," I said, turning toward him. "A painting called—"

I broke off abruptly, unable to continue when I saw the small scar on his neck. Nearly an inch long, the scar tissue rose off the skin, red and wormlike, just beneath his jaw line.

"What is it?" he asked.

"Let's go back in the office," I said.

When we were inside I closed the door.

"The scar on your neck," I said. "How recent is that?"

He shrugged, his whole demeanor changing, as if he were shrinking in on himself.

"You feel like talking about it?" I asked.

"How do you know about it?" he asked, his eyes moistening.

"I'm trying to find out who's doing it," I said.

He shook his head. "It's the worst thing that's ever happened to me in my entire life. By a long shot."

"Where'd it happen?" I asked.

"In Medical. I was just going to get a snack out of the vending machine from the break room in the back. It was supper time and the sandwich I brought just wasn't enough. He jumped me from behind. I never saw him."

"No one was in the infirmary or the nurses' station?"

"If they were they didn't say or do anything," he said,

anger at the edge of his voice.

His breathing became more erratic and his chin quivered.

"He tackled me. Grabbed a handful of my hair and slammed my face onto the tile floor over and over again. Broke my nose, chipped my tooth—this one's a crown," he added, pointing to one of his front teeth. "He was so strong. Pinned me to the floor with his whole body, pressing down on me so hard I couldn't breathe, I couldn't move. I tried. I tried so hard to get away, but I couldn't. I was dazed, maybe even unconscious a moment."

He paused, trying to regain control. I waited, nodding in an attempt to be reassuring.

"He kept whispering," he said, looking down at the ground. "The whole time. Just whispering. I could feel his hot breath on my ear. God, it drove me crazy. It was almost the worst part. That and what he made me do to myself."

I reached out and put my hand on his shoulder. He jumped when he felt it, but recovered quickly, then put his hand on mine and patted it. It was something no man had ever done in all my years of comforting and counseling the broken and bereaved.

"Have you talked to anybody about it?" I asked.

He shook his head.

"Would you be willing to?"

He gave me a small shrug. "Who?"

"How about Ms. Lopez?"

"How about you?"

"Sure."

"I was so scared," he said. "I thought he was going to kill me. You think you'd rather die than have some sick prick butt fuck you on the floor—until you're in the situation. Then all you can think about is surviving, doing whatever it takes to stay alive. I did just what he told me. He said if I did, not only would he let me live, but he wouldn't rape me."

I nodded, trying to reassure him and encourage him to

continue.

Several inmates had stopped what they had been doing and were now staring at Sandy. They couldn't hear what he was saying, but they could see how upset he was—something that excited the predators who were always looking for a vulnerability to exploit. I felt like we should move, continue this in a more private place, but didn't want to interrupt his cathartic flow.

"He made me hold my hand behind me," he said. "Took my index finger in his mouth in a very sexual way, then he told me to finger myself or he'd slit my throat and fuck me up the ass while I bled to death."

He hesitated a moment, took in a deep breath and let it out slowly.

"I did it," he said. "I did that to myself. I would've done anything. There are worse things I thought. Far worse. Better me than him, right?"

I nodded.

"He then took the shank away from my throat and gripped my larynx so hard I thought he was going to crush it and made me stick the butt of the shank up my . . . up into . . . my . . . self. And I did it. He said that's all I had to do and he'd let me go, so I did it."

I waited for a long moment but he seemed to be finished.

"I'm so sorry," I said. "No one should ever have to endure anything like that. I'm so, so sorry."

He nodded and gave me a tight-lipped half smile.

We were quiet a long time. I walked over and stood near the front of the office next to the glass and stared at the gawking inmates until one by one they returned to what they were doing before they saw blood in the water.

"You okay?" I asked when I turned back toward him.

He nodded and really seemed like he was.

"Feel like answering a couple of questions?"

He narrowed his eyes and nodded very deliberately. "If it'll help you catch and castrate him."

"You sure it was a shank?"

"Positive. It was homemade. I could feel it. It had tape on the handle and it was sharp underneath it. Even with the tape it cut me."

I tried not to wince.

"You get a look at him? Any part of him? His hands? Arms? Anything?"

He shook his head. "He put some kind of hood over my head. I didn't see anything. You think if I did he'd be breathing without a machine right now?"

I understood how he felt, but such sentiments coming from someone so soft spoken and gentle sounded hollow and kind of sad.

"Did he have a smell you can remember?" I asked. "A certain sound? Did he use poor grammar? Could you tell what race he was? How old?"

He closed his eyes, seeming to strain to put himself back into his nightmare.

"He had a fruity smell, sort of citrusy, like orange or lime-scented lotion," he said. "And his breath smelled of coffee. I've always pictured him as a young white guy, but don't know why."

I nodded and neither of us said anything for a long while, just sat there in the psychic reverberations the recounting of such a traumatic experience had produced.

"I'm sorry I had to ask about it," I said, "but the information will help us catch him."

"You're not going to tell anyone, are you?" he said, his voice pleading.

"No," I said. "I'm not."

A touch of relief seemed to relax him a little.

"This helped," he said. "Can I come talk to you again sometime if I need to?"

"Of course. Anytime."

He stood and handed me all three Dalì books. "Just take these. Keep 'em as long as you need."

I stood and took the books. "Thanks," I said. "I'll bring them back soon."

When I reached the door and was about to open it, he said, "Chaplain, you know all that stuff he made me do to myself?"

"Yeah," I said.

"I did everything he told me to."

I nodded.

"And when I had done every last thing he told me to he raped me anyway."

Chapter Eighteen

I had the Dalí book on the desk in front of me, opened to the painting "Young Virgin Autosodomized by her Own Chastity" when DeLisa Lopez walked into my office.

"What's that?" she asked.

"Salvador Dalí painting," I said. "What the rapist is doing reminded me of it."

She leaned over the desk to study the painting. I turned the book toward her so she could see it better.

In the Surrealist painting of subconscious shapes juxtaposed with recognizable ones, a young woman with wavy blond hair, naked except for sheer seamed stockings and 1950s-style black patent ballerina shoes, is leaning out of a window-like box, holding herself up by a dancer's bar. Several horn-shaped objects are floating around, two of them merging with her butt cheeks, one directly behind her upturned rear end ready for penetration.

The caption on the page next to the painting quotes Dalí saying, "The horn of the rhinoceros, at one time the uniceros, is in reality the horn of the legendary unicorn, the symbol of chastity. A young virgin can rely on it, or play moral games with it, as well as she would have done in the days of courtly love."

"Bizarre," Lisa said. "But most of his stuff is, isn't it?"

"I like Dalí," I said.

"You do?"

I nodded.

She looked back down at the painting. "I can see why it made you think of our sicko."

"If you're going to use psychological jargon I won't be able to keep up," I said.

She smiled.

"So what does it mean?" she asked, nodding toward the image.

I shrugged. "I'm not sure exactly."

She gave me a wide-eyed expression beneath arching brows as she sat down in the chair across from me.

"You just gonna sit and stare at the picture until it comes to you?" she asked.

"It would have already if you hadn't interrupted me."

She smiled again. "Sorry."

"Since you're here," I said, "how about answering a few more questions."

"It'd make me feel better about interrupting such important investigative work," she said. "Did you talk to Dil?"

I nodded.

"And?"

"And I have some more questions for you," I said.

"Sorry," she said. "Shoot."

"How many men would you say have confided in you about this?" I asked.

Her eyes narrowed and she looked up toward the ceiling. "I'm not sure exactly. Five maybe—but they've all told me there are others."

"Why haven't you reported it?" I asked, the surprise showing in my voice.

Like me, she was required by law to report all crimes or plans to commit crimes.

"Wasn't sure I even believed the first couple," she said. "They wouldn't submit to a physical. I thought they might be lying—especially since it was the same story. Then the next couple made me swear I wouldn't and their confidence in me is more important than me keeping my job. Besides, I told you and you'll catch him."

"And they all told pretty much the same story?"

She nodded.

"Did they all have a mark on their neck?"

She nodded again. "They call it the mark of the beast."

"That would have been helpful to know," I said.

"Sorry," she said.

"After they did what he told them to," I said, "to themselves, did he rape them anyway?"

She shook her head. "If he did they didn't say so."

"None of them?"

"None. I got the feeling the guy's impotent."

I thought about it.

"Why?" she asked.

"I talked to a victim who said he did everything the guy told him to and he still raped him."

"Who talked to you?" she asked.

I frowned at her. "I can't say."

"Right," she said. "Well, maybe he's able to sometimes. And maybe some or all of the men I'm seeing are lying about that part of it."

"Maybe," I said. "Were your guys all attacked in the same place or various locations?"

She pursed her lips as she thought about it. "Different places."

"The guy I talked to said it happened in the back hallway of Medical."

"Well now, wait a minute," she said.

"What?"

"Hold on," she said. "I'm thinking."

She narrowed her eyes in concentrated thought again, but looked down instead of up.

"They did all happen in or around or very close to the medical building," she said. "One was the greenhouse, one was near Confinement—both of those are right behind Medical—two were in Classification—and that's the other side of the same building. I think the other was in the infirmary."

I nodded, thinking about what it meant.

"So it's Medical, right?"

"It certainly sounds like the place to start," I said. "What about the times it happened? Were they all at a similar time?"

She shrugged. "I'm not sure," she said. "I can probably find out. Is it important?"

Chapter Nineteen

With very few exceptions, African-Americans in Pottersville lived in one small part of town—one still referred to by many as the Quarters.

Poverty was part of life in a small town like Pottersville. There were very few good jobs, very few opportunities of any kind. But it was far worse for the small percentage of black men and women for whom inequality and disenfranchisement, living without in the land of plenty, was a way of life—and had been for generations.

Over the past few years, as despair had increased so had the abuse of alcohol and drugs. More and more meth labs were being found, more and more young men were going to prison. The senselessness and hopelessness, the raw futility, was overwhelming.

Dad was campaigning this afternoon, courting the black vote, and had asked me to meet him near Merrill's mom's house. By the time I arrived, I was depressed and disgusted.

I was driving a tricked-out black 1985 Chevrolet Monte Carlo SS with T-tops, red pinstriping, a V-8 engine with a four-speed automatic transmission, a six-inch lift kit with twenty-six-inch chrome rims, a trunk full of speakers, illegally dark tinted windows, and a loud dual exhaust system.

It had been seized in a large drug bust and would soon be auctioned off by the sheriff's department, but until then it was on loan to me. Dad's justification was that I was consulting on the case and that I had destroyed my vehicle while attempting to stop an inmate escape. It still seemed like a dangerous thing to do during an election year but he assured me it wouldn't be an issue. And at the moment I didn't have a lot of options.

He had the screen door open and was stepping off her front porch when I pulled up behind his car, and met me by the time I got out.

"You look like a drug dealer," he said.

"Already been pulled over three times," I said. "You ought to see the looks on their faces when they see a white man in a clerical collar."

He smiled.

We were quiet a moment, already beginning to sweat.

"We got the prelim back today," he said.

I raised my eyebrows, inviting him to continue.

"Our vic wasn't lynched," he said.

"Well, yes he was," I said.

"I mean that's not what killed him," he said. "He was dead long before he was hanged."

I nodded, thinking about it.

Unlike most of the dilapidated clapboard houses and faded single-wide trailers with multiple satellite dishes on them, Ma Monroe had a red brick home with freshly painted trim. In contrast to the trash, discarded appliances, and shiny pimped-out luxury cars in many of the other yards, hers was clean and neatly manicured with a modest mid-sized Ford—all of which Merrill was responsible for.

"Cause of death?" I asked.

"He was beaten to death," he said. "He had massive blunt force trauma. His liver was lacerated, his spleen ruptured, and he had an acute subdural hematoma."

I thought about it some more.

"I think whoever killed him wanted it to look like something other than what it was," he said. "Hang a black man from a tree and everybody automatically assumes it's racially motivated, that it's a mob or the Klan. Be a smart thing to do no matter who the killer is. Be brilliant if he's black."

I nodded.

As we stood there near the street, Dad waved to every vehicle that passed by—whether log truck or gold-trimmed SUV with spinning rims. Not his usual understated wave, but his big I'm-your-best-friend politician wave. I felt self-conscious and embarrassed, and I questioned why he had asked me to meet him here, which added guilt to the other experiences I was having.

From an early age, I had been as comfortable around black people as white, and I was sensitive to and angered by the rampant racism in Pottersville. It was probably due in part to the fact that the woman who cared for me during my most formative years was black, partly because of my relationship with Merrill, and perhaps partly because of an innate and intense hatred of injustice, but it had separated and at times even alienated me from my family.

My parents were of the "you can work with them, even be casual friends with them, but shouldn't get too close to or even think about dating or marrying them" generation. Their formative years were prior to the Civil Rights movement. They were in school at the time of integration. Much of the conflict Dad and I had during my teenage years was related to my anger at his subtle and not so subtle racism. He was different now, having rid himself of much of the residual racism still present in Jake, but he still wasn't as accepted or as comfortable as I was among the people of color of Pottersville, and I wondered if he had asked me to meet him out here because he wanted to remind them that I was his son.

"We should have a more complete autopsy in a day or two."

He could have told me all of this on the phone. Maybe I was right about why he had asked me here.

"Still no ID?" I asked.

He shook his head. "If he's in the system we'll have it in a few days. If he's not . . . I don't know what we'll do."

I looked over at the old white wooden AME church on the other side of Ma Monroe's house. It was small and leaning, and needed to be painted, its tiny steeple spotted gray and black with mildew. I shivered slightly when I looked at the woods beyond it and thought of the horror it held for Merrill.

"Do you know anything about a preacher from Marianna being killed back in those woods?" I asked.

His eyes narrowed, his expression one of alarm. "What? When?"

"Ever," I said. "But specifically twenty-nine or thirty years ago."

"No," he said, shaking his head. "Why?"

"Merrill saw him get killed when he was little."

He shook his head. "I was a deputy back then. I would've known about it."

"Not if it was never reported."

"True. He would've been, what, three or four? He sure?"

I nodded.

"I'll check into it," he said, "but I can't imagine it hasn't come out by now if there was anything to it."

"If Merrill says he saw it . . . "

"I'll look into and let you know," he said. "Speaking of Merrill . . . I need your help."

My eyebrows shot up.

"I need you and him to help me with the black vote," he said. "Would you talk to him?"

I hesitated. He was putting me in an awkward position. I hated politics and I felt uncomfortable even asking Merrill for his own vote, much less to work on Dad's behalf, but there was no way I could refuse this man who had done so much for me for so long, no way I could not do all I could to help him in any way I could.

"If you don't," he said, "I'm going to lose the election."

Chapter Twenty

Ordinarily Carla and I had Rudy's to ourselves late at night, but with rotating teams of officers and deputies searching for the escaped inmate around the clock, the cowbell above the door kept clanging, the jukebox kept playing, and the coffee pot kept emptying.

I wasn't even sure why I came. Carla didn't need looking out for now that she was no longer spending all night every night alone in an open diner on the side of a rural highway, but here I was again, walking through the door at a little after nine.

Rudy's Diner served Southern fried food just like all the no-name cafés in small Southern towns, but it didn't look like one. With stools and a counter fronting a grill and booths next to plate glass windows it looked more like a welfare Waffle House than anything else.

Jake and Fred Goodwin were in a booth in the back on the opposite side of the restaurant from the booth I considered mine. I was sure they had just come in from the woods and were probably talking about the search or the weather— anything but the election, but it looked conspiratorial, as if Jake were somehow betraying Dad.

Next to them four men I recognized from the prison but didn't know were laughing loudly when not shoveling grits, eggs, bacon, and toast into their mouths. Across the room, Carla's boyfriend slouched in a booth with a group of guys his age,

their posture conveying how bored they were with life. Todd
and Shane sat in a booth next to them, and at the counter in
the center Sandy Hartman sat alone, his head down, shoulders
hunched, sipping coffee.

Beyond him, Carla, hair fallen, face drawn, fatigue
obvious, was balancing plates on her hands and arms. She gave
me a half smile, then looked away. As she carried the food over
to Todd and Shane, I walked over to Sandy.

"How's it going?" I asked.

He looked up at me, squinting against the light above us,
frowned, and shrugged. "It's going."

I waited for him to elaborate but he didn't.

"You okay?"

His eyes widened and locked on mine. He then
glanced around the room to see if anyone was witnessing our
interaction.

"I'm just fine. Thanks. You?"

It was a dismissal.

I nodded then walked over toward my booth, nodding
to Carla's boyfriend, Cody Gaskin, and his friends as I did. They
didn't respond.

I stopped at Todd and Shane's table.

"You gotta concentrate to be that cool," Todd said,
looking at the boys. "Can't be distracted by nodding or
speaking."

I smiled.

What made that funny was the way Todd was just like
them when he was that age and wasn't that much different now.

Looking down at Todd and Shane I realized again how
much alike they looked.

Todd and Shane had thick necks, crew cuts, and even
sitting, bowed out their chests and flexed their muscles against
the tight, too small T-shirts they wore. Completing their look of
pseudo-soldier, their camouflage fatigues were tucked into their
black tactical boots.

There was one big difference though. Shane was nearly twice the size of Todd. It was as if Todd was a smaller version of Shane, a to-scale model that maintained the exact proportions in miniature. They even had identical razor wire armband tattoos around their right biceps.

The boys were talking so low it sounded like whispering, but occasionally I heard a string of words well enough to make out most of a sentence. "If I caught one throwin' my bitch a bone I'd damn sure do it."

Shane was saying something but I was too distracted for it to register.

"How often you tappin' that ass, man? She looks like she can hardly walk."

Before I realized what I was doing I had stepped back over to their table.

"That's because of how tired she is," I said. "And if I ever hear any of you say anything like that about her again, you'll be walking funny for the rest of your little lives. Promise you that."

"Shit, man, chill out," one of them said.

He was a pale, pimply faced boy with a bad haircut and wounded, angry eyes.

"Stop it, Sean," a boy I recognized from the football team said. "Just stop."

But Sean couldn't.

"I's just kiddin'," Sean said. "Besides, I wasn't talkin' to you."

"But I am talking to you," I said. "And you better listen."

"We hear you, okay?" the other guy who wasn't Cody said. "He's a dick. We're sorry. We won't let him say anything like that again."

"Okay?" Sean said. "So will you leave us the fuck alone now?"

Cody had yet to utter a sound or look me in the eye.

I stared at him.

After a few moments of him refusing to look at me, I shook my head and walked back over to Todd and Shane's table.

"What's wrong with him?" Shane said.

I looked back at the boys who were now dropping their napkins on the table, preparing to leave.

"No, him," he said, nodding over at Sandy. "Somethin' just ain't right with him."

That was another difference. Shane did most of the talking.

I followed his gaze over to Sandy, who had stood up and was dropping a few bills on the counter. He leaned over slightly as if from an unseen weight pressing down on him, and moved slowly like someone terminally ill or deeply depressed.

"Not a team player," Todd added.

"Whatta you think it is?" I asked, trying to sound casual.

"Told you," Todd said. "He's a quitter."

"Hell if I know," Shane said. "Don't know that much about women."

"I've heard that," I said.

Todd laughed.

I looked back at Shane.

"He quit SAR?"

He nodded.

"Any idea why?"

He shook his head.

"Still no sign of the inmate?" I asked.

He frowned and shook his head, then rubbed his hand across his military haircut. "We'll get him."

Todd nodded. "Hopefully before he kills anybody else."

"You think Jensen killed the man at the river?" I asked.

He nodded. "And he's wearing his clothes right now trying to hitch a ride somewhere."

"Or hiding out until things die down," Shane said, "and then gonna hop a ride outta here."

That gave me an idea, and I made a mental note to talk

to Dad about it.

After a few more forced comments our conversation dwindled and I made my way to my booth in the back. As I sat down Cody and his posse stood up and slowly walked out of the diner without paying, a couple of them glaring at me as they did.

Carla said something to Cody but he kept walking.

Cody and his friends reminded me of Todd and Shane and so many other guys around here—especially those in law enforcement—and I wondered what it was about small Southern towns that turned out misogynistic young men with such regularity and proficiency. Equally confounding were the mothers who raised such sons and the young women who were attracted to them.

"I'm so worried about him," Carla said.

I had been staring at the door, thinking, and didn't realize she was standing beside me. I looked up at her and gave her a weak smile.

"I'm worried about you," I said.

"He's usually very good to me," she said. "Something happened. Last week he was gone for three days—just disappeared. Nobody knew where he was—including his dad. When he showed up again, he wouldn't say where'd he'd been or what he'd been doing, and he's so different now. Something happened."

"Any idea what?" I asked.

She thought about it for a minute, pursing her lips, then shook her head. "Would you talk to him?"

"Me?"

"Yeah. You're so good at—"

"He's not a fan and it'll probably make things worse, but if you want me to . . ."

"It's hard to imagine it being any worse."

"At what point will you walk away?" I asked.

She shrugged. "I don't know."

I shook my head. "I know how—"

The bell above the door sounded and we both turned to see Anna walk in.

"Tell you what," Carla said. "I'll walk away from Cody when you walk away from her."

Chapter Twenty-one

Carla had compared her two-month relationship with her boyfriend to my over two-decade obsession with Anna. It was surprisingly teenage girlish of her, but I understood what she meant. The hopeless hope love inspires isn't easy to surrender even after two minutes.

Would I ever be able to walk away from Anna? Would I ever be free of the notion that the fates would finally relent and look with favor on us? Probably not, as long as the slightest wisp of hope remained.

As Anna crossed the room toward me, I wondered how my life might be different if we were together. Circumstances— some of them far beyond my control—had ended my marriage twice, but I wondered if Susan and I might somehow still be together if I hadn't held in reserve some small part of my heart for Anna.

I hadn't thought of Susan lately. Our marriage ended badly the first time—worse the second, but I wondered how she was doing. Was she remarried? She had never been good at being alone. Did she have kids? A pain of guilt and regret ran through me as I thought about our child that might have been.

"You don't look too happy to see me," Anna said.

"Actually, thoughts of just how happy I am to see you led to darker, troubling, unhappy thoughts."

"I can tell," she said. "Wanna talk about it?"

I shook my head.

"Sure?"

I nodded.

She slid into the booth across from me, a clean, fresh, slightly fruity fragrance following her, filling the air around us, and before I realized what I was doing, I started breathing a little more deeply, as if trying to inhale her.

As I gazed into her infinitely deep brown eyes, I wondered how much of my life I had spent doing that. I thought about all we had shared since childhood, all we knew about the other, all our eyes had witnessed of the other's life, all the words our mouths had spoken, our ears had heard, all we had perceived of the other's silence.

Carla walked over with a pot of coffee and a couple of cups. As she filled my cup, she said, "Y'all want anything to eat?"

I shook my head.

"No thanks," Anna said. "And can I just have water?"

"Sure," she said, then paused for a moment to consider her. "You look tired."

"I am," Anna said.

When Carla went to retrieve the glass of water, I said, "You still look great."

Her face lit up and her eyes moistened. "Only because you're looking through the eyes of love."

"Without denying that's what I'm doing," I said, "I refuse to concede that what I said is anything but absolute and objective truth."

While getting Anna's water, Carla had to stop to checkout Todd and Shane and the other group of correctional officers. When she brought the water to the table, only Anna and I and Jake and Fred remained in the restaurant.

"Jake's eating with the enemy, isn't he?" Anna asked.

"What are they talking about?" I asked Carla.

"You know I can't reveal what clients say," she said with

a smile. "And you of all people should be glad I can't."

"Know his secrets, do you?" Anna asked.

"Just the incriminating ones," she said.

"The only ones worth knowing," Anna said.

"Why don't you go try to get some sleep," I said to Carla. "I'll take Jake's money, and we can wait on anyone else who comes in."

Anna nodded vigorously. "John can't even make coffee, but I'm hell in the kitchen. Get some rest."

"Y'all sure?"

"I insist."

"Thanks," she said. "Come get me if you need anything."

Carla lived with Rudy in the back of the diner in a small area she normally tried to avoid, but by this time Rudy would be passed out in front of the TV, a long since emptied bottle of vodka on the floor beside his chair.

As Carla walked behind the counter, she took off her apron and hung it on a hook next to the back door. After saying something to Jake and pointing to the coffee pot, she turned back toward us. "And Anna."

"Yeah?"

"John has something important he needs to tell you," she said.

She then smiled at me and disappeared into the back.

"You do?" she said.

I shook my head. "She's trying to be funny."

We fell silent a moment. I drank my coffee. Anna sipped her water and made a face. "I always forget Rudy's water comes straight from the tap."

"But it's the chlorine-laced sulfur that gives it flavor," I said.

I slid my saucer and cup toward her.

She shook her head. "No thanks."

"Try it," I said. "Bitterness completely covers the sulfur and chlorine."

She smiled.

I smiled.

We were still smiling when Jake and Fred walked over.

"I was just telling Jake the first thing I'm going to do when I'm sheriff is offer you a job," Fred said in his deep, rich voice.

Beneath his thick silver hair, Fred Goodwin's ice-blue eyes were intense and bloodshot, etched with lines nearly as red as his fleshy sun-kissed face.

"I told him you'd make a good dog catcher," Jake said.

I looked over at Jake in mock surprise. "When did your opinion of me increase so much?"

"Guess it was the way you stopped that inmate from escaping," he said.

"You think we'll catch him?" Fred asked.

By far the oldest member of search and rescue, he was also the most polished, his suave manner making him well-suited for politics.

I was reminded of the thought I had earlier because of what Shane had said, and wanted to mention it to Jake, but not in front of Fred. I decided to wait and mention it to Dad later.

I nodded toward Jake. "We've got the best and the brightest working on it."

"You're right about that," he said. "Well you folks have a good night."

When they left and we were finally alone we both sighed simultaneously.

"How long you think it'll be before the next shift arrives?" she asked.

"Not nearly long enough."

She frowned and nodded. "As much as I'd like to delay what I need to say, just so we could stay like this a little longer, I better go ahead and say it."

My heart started racing and I braced myself for what was coming. She sounded too ominous for it to be good.

I waited.

She took in a deep breath and let it out slowly. "I've been so unfair to you. I honestly didn't realize just how unfair until recently."

"By withholding sex?" I said.

She tried to smile, but couldn't. That's when I knew I was in real trouble.

"Sorry," I said. "Defensive humor."

She nodded, her expression one of understanding.

"You really haven't been able to move on with your life because of me," she said.

"That's hardly your fault," I said, my throat constricting, my voice dry and pinched.

"I haven't wanted you to. And it's not just that I haven't encouraged you to. I've actually tried to prevent you from it. Waiting for . . . what? Something to happen to Chris? For you to give me an ultimatum?"

Whatever it was she was waiting for, I had been waiting for the same thing, and now she was telling me what I was waiting for wasn't going to come.

"I've known all along what I was doing," she said. "I just hadn't realized until recently how spectacularly unfair it was of me."

There was a finality to her words and the way she was saying them. She had come here to release me, to cut the unseen strings that bound me to her, to give me what she believed she had withheld from me. It didn't matter that I didn't want to be free. It didn't matter that I never felt she was being the slightest bit unfair to me.

"What brought about this epiphany?" I asked.

"Does it matter?" she asked. "It's true, isn't it? I've imprisoned you."

"I've imprisoned myself. But what was it?"

She shook her head.

"I want to know," I said. "There's got to be a reason for

my release."

"I'm sorry," she said.

"For what?"

"I'm pregnant."

Chapter Twenty-two

After the paper mill in Port St. Joe had closed and the largest private landholder in the state had become its biggest developer, the small community at the mouth of St. Joseph Bay began to change. With the pungent, acrid odor and thick smoky fog of the mill a thing of the past and land once reserved for slash pines released, wealthy people from Atlanta began to pay unimaginable sums of money for a sliver of sand close to the Gulf. The powers that be thought they had seen the future, and the future they saw was tourism.

Gift shops, restaurants, real estate offices, and banks began to pop up downtown, and as many of the tags on the cars were from Alabama and Georgia as from Florida—most of them luxury SUVs.

Lifelong residents had sold their family homes, quadrupling their money, and moved to areas with more reasonable property tax rates. Man had come to the forest and money had come to town, and nothing would ever be the same for the land or the people of what once was the forgotten coast.

And then came the housing bubble bust, followed by the financial sector crash, then a full-on recession.

Everything had slowed, even stopped for a while, but now, several years later, there were signs of life again.

Next to the yachts and large fishing boats that filled the revitalized marina, Rachel Mills and I were in the Dockside Café sitting on high stools at a tall wooden table with a view of

the bay. The window was open and through it blew the warm
bay breeze and the soothing sounds of seagulls and sailboat
riggings—all swirling around in a muffling din of waves and
wind.

I had the fried shrimp basket with fries, she had the
oysters with onion rings, and we both had sweet tea with lime.

Gazing at the setting sun sinking into the bay, she said,
"No wonder people are paying small fortunes to have a place
here."

"Never thought I'd miss the paper mill," I said.

"Don't tell me you're not in favor of progress."

I didn't say anything.

"Well?" she asked, her brows rising over her pale blue
eyes.

"You said not to tell you."

She smiled.

"I can tell you that most of what people are sold as
progress, isn't," I said.

We were quiet a moment, our gazes drifting back out to
the bay. A charter boat was pulling into the marina, its red-faced
passengers windblown and weary.

Anna is pregnant.

I had tried so hard to put that out of my mind, to
suppress it, hide it, bury it beneath even my subconscious, but
nothing was working—at least not for very long.

Push it back down. Now is not the time. Forget it. Let it
go.

But that's it. All hope is gone—even the last tiny sliver I
was holding in reserve.

Her news had finally and completely ended us once and
for all with a finality and certainty nothing else could.

"This is nice," she said.

"Huh?" I said, coming back to the present moment,
aware of sitting across from Rachel again.

"Thanks for bringing me," she said. "Can't believe we

haven't talked about the case."

"We will."

"When?"

"How about now?" I asked, pushing back my basket and thoughts of Anna.

She laughed. "Fine by me. I know I'm expected to put out."

She ate one more onion ring and shoved her basket next to mine in the center of the table.

"Still no ID?"

She shook her head.

"That mean there's not going to be one?"

"We could still get a hit. If we don't have one by the first of next week, I'd say we'll have to get it another way. We've already got people looking at missing persons reports. We'll figure out who he is sooner or later."

"Dad only had very preliminary autopsy results," I said. "Got anything to add?"

"The victim had water in his lungs," she said.

I thought about that. In itself it didn't mean anything.

I said, "Cause of death the same?"

She shrugged. "ME says the water could have gotten in the lungs after he was dead or while sustaining his other injuries. Just no way to know for sure."

I nodded.

Our waitress came back, picked up our baskets and napkins, refilled our teas, and dropped off the check.

"You think Jensen killed him?" she asked.

I shrugged.

"There's just not enough in his file to go on," she said. "And it's always what's not in there that tells us whether or not they're even capable of it."

"Well," I said, glancing up at the clock, "if you're not opposed to mixing a little business with pleasure, let's go find out."

Chapter Twenty-three

The Gulf/Franklin Center was an extension of Gulf
Coast State College that saved students from Port St. Joe,
Apalachicola, and Carrabelle from driving over an hour into
Panama City to the main campus. Through the use of adjuncts,
video, and professors willing to drive over, the center offered
a wide variety of classes, though it would be difficult to
complete a degree. Its two strongest programs were nursing and
correctional officer training—professions in high demand in
Florida and programs you could complete without traveling to
the main campus.

When we arrived at the center the students milling about
the entrances let me know we had arrived during one of their
breaks. Without checking in at the office, we went straight into
Tracy Jensen's classroom and found her talking to a student.
They were the only two people in the room.

The nervous student, who probably made straight As,
was seeking clarification on a writing assignment. While we
waited I glanced around the room. Based on the notes on the
dry marker board, the introductory psyche class Tracy taught
was covering psychological disorders and what the various
approaches, such as humanistic, behavioral, and cognitive, said
about their cause, diagnosis, and treatment. Both the front
and back walls of the room were formed by folding partitions.
Before rows of narrow tables and plastic chairs, a metal podium

on wheels had a textbook opened on it.

The student could tell Tracy Jensen was distracted by our presence and quickly stumbled over her words as she nervously finished up.

"Can I help you?" Tracy asked the moment the student finished.

She was an extremely thin white woman with wispy blond hair and sunken cheeks. She wore a nice enough business suit but her well-worn shoes were poorly made and didn't quite match the rest of her outfit.

"Is there somewhere we can talk?" I asked.

"I was just about to go get a Coke," the student said, and made a quick exit.

"I'm in the middle of a class," Tracy said. "What's this about?"

"Your brother," I said.

She began shaking her head immediately, anger flaring in her pinched face. "I don't want to—"

"I'm the chaplain of PCI," I said. "And I just—"

"Did they kill him?" she asked. "Is he dead?"

"No," I said. "Who's 'they'?"

"Why're you here?"

"I'm trying to find out why he ran," I said, "where he might go, and how to get him back without anyone getting hurt."

"You've got to know that even if I knew something I wouldn't tell you, but the truth is I don't know."

The students beginning to trickle back into the room were a mixture of middle-aged women and college-aged coeds. With the exception of a few who had obviously come from work, they were all dressed very casually—shorts, T-shirts, and flip-flops, many of the young girls with extremely short shorts made of soft material that looked like pajama bottoms.

"You know more than we do," I said.

"Obviously," she said.

I looked over at Rachel and smiled.

"I mean I know enough not to barge into the middle of a professor's lecture," she said.

"Oh, we know that," I said. "We came during one of your breaks."

"I can't do this right now," she said. "You'll have to excuse me."

"Why don't you show a video and step out into the hall with us for a minute?"

She glanced at the TV, then back at me, her eyes narrowed. Retrieving the remote from within the podium, she pointed it toward the TV and pressed a button.

"Go ahead and start the video," she said to the class. "I'll be back in just a moment. I'm going to leave the lights on so you can take notes. The test will include all the material on the video so make sure you get it."

She walked out into the hallway. We followed.

"You say you want to help Michael," she said when she had closed the door, "but it's a little late for that now. Where were you when he needed you before all this happened?"

"He's your best chance of getting back your brother without him getting hurt," Rachel said, nodding toward me.

"What did he need help with?" I asked.

The doors at the end of the hallway opened and a tall, thin black man in a light blue sports shirt with his name and GCSC stitched on it came in. He held a bottle of cleaning solution in one hand and a rag in the other.

"I'm not going to do this here," she whispered.

The man entered the classroom closest to us and turned on the lights, leaving the door open behind him.

"Has he contacted you?" I asked.

She shook her head. "I'm not saying anything else. I'm going back into my classroom and if you interrupt me again I'll call campus security and have you removed."

I knew there was no way a campus this size had security,

but when she turned and walked into her classroom I didn't try
to stop her.

"That went well," Rachel said.

I shrugged. "About as well as I expected. Come on."

"Where we going now?"

"Across the campus to talk to her mother."

Chapter Twenty-four

Unlike Tracy Jensen, her mother, Wanda, was warm and friendly. We found her cleaning the large classroom used by the nursing program. In addition to the usual tables, chairs, and podium, it had built-in cabinets and drawers for supplies, a sink, and room on the side for two hospital beds. Simulating a hospital room, the beds were separated by a curtain and held resuscitation dummies hooked to empty IVs.

Like the tall, thin African-American man from the other building, Wanda wore a light blue sports shirt with GCSC and her name embroidered on it. The shirt was untucked, its tail resting on the navy blue jogging bottoms covering her large backside and thighs. She was on her hands and knees scraping something off the floor when we walked in.

When she glanced back at us she smiled, and stood, which took a while and required the use of a nearby table and chair.

"Lot easier to get down," she said.

I thought about the book on the fabric of the universe I had been listening to, and how it had described gravity as warps and wrinkles in space-time like a wooden floor with water damage.

"Gravity gets the best of all of us," I said.

"Yeah but some of us have more mass than others," she said. "Still, drop me and my anorexic daughter off the Empire

State Building, we'd hit the ground at the same time."

I must have looked a little surprised, because she smiled and said, "I'm reading a book on the fabric of the cosmos to my husband. He's legally blind but loves books like that, so he's giving me an education."

"I'm reading the same book," I said. "Well, listening to it."

"Do you understand it?" she asked.

"Only some," I said.

She smiled. "I know. Used to think I was somewhat smart until I started reading all this bucket stuff."

I smiled. I loved being surprised. It was refreshing.

"Bucket?" Rachel asked.

"Something about if there were nothing in the universe—no planets, stars, or people—would the contents of a spinning bucket feel any effects."

Rachel looked confused.

"Is the universe a something or a nothing," I explained.

Wanda smiled.

"If you take all the letters out of the alphabet," I said, "would there still be an alphabet?"

Rachel shook her head.

"Once you get it all figured out," I said to Wanda, "you can explain it to me. I'm John Jordan, by the way. I'm—"

"I know. Your daddy's the sheriff of Potter County and you're the chaplain at the prison."

I nodded. "This is Rachel Mills from FDLE. We're trying to find Michael."

She shook her head and I thought she was about to shut down, but she said, "I don't know what that boy was thinking. Just about to get out and he does a damn fool thing like that."

"There had to be a good reason," I said. "Any idea what it might be?"

She shook her head.

"If you know, you need to tell us," Rachel said, her voice

harsh and demanding. "We're his best hope of—"

"If I knew I would," she said.

I looked at Rachel with narrowed eyes and shook my head.

"Sorry," she said to Wanda. "Your daughter wasn't helpful and made it clear she didn't ever intend to be."

"My daughter's under a lot of pressure. 'Course she puts it on herself. She's very hard on herself. Doesn't feel as though she can relax or let her guard down. Not even for a minute. She feels she has so much to overcome, to prove."

"Why?" Rachel asked.

I knew the answer and was hoping Rachel wouldn't ask the question.

"Because," Wanda said, "her father's a cripple, her brother's in prison, and her mother's a janitor."

I thought about how much more comfortable Wanda was with herself than Tracy. She had nothing to prove, nothing to apologize for, no agendas or motives. She just was. And it was a thing of beauty. How does a mother like Wanda have a daughter like Tracy?

"What I've seen," I said, "her mother's the best thing going for her."

She smiled. "Thank you."

"Nothing happened with you or your husband that might make Michael think he had to get out now, did it?" I asked.

She shook her head. "Nothing has changed. Things are very difficult for us—financially I mean. We can't afford to live here anymore. We'll probably move up to Pottersville. Somewhere like that. Might be your neighbors. But we've always been poor, and I haven't said anything to Michael."

"What about a girlfriend?" I asked.

"If he has one I don't know anything about it."

"If he contacted you or came to see you would you tell us?" Rachel asked.

She shook her head again. "No. Probably wouldn't."

This was a direct contradiction of what she had said earlier, but I didn't say anything.

"So he could be hiding at your house right now and you wouldn't report him?"

She nodded. "That's right," she said. "But he's not. You're welcome to check."

"We will," Rachel said.

"No we won't," I said.

"Don't get me wrong, Ms. Mills," Wanda said, "I'd try to talk Michael into turning himself in, but I wouldn't turn him in. I couldn't."

"I understand," I said. "If you think of anything, please let us know. You can reach me through the prison or the sheriff's department anytime."

"I will," she said. "Michael talked very highly of you. Please find him. Please don't let anybody hurt him. He'll have had a good reason for running. Bet my soul on it. Please find him before anybody else do. I don't want some trigger-happy kid to kill my boy."

Chapter Twenty-five

"**I** still can't believe you made me ride in this thing," Rachel said.

We were getting back into the pimped-out Monte Carlo in the mostly empty Gulf/Franklin Center parking lot.

"Hate the game not the player," I said with a smile.

She laughed.

When I cranked the car and turned on the headlights, I could see Wanda Jensen's coworker walking toward us. I cut the lights, switched off the car, and Rachel and I got out.

"That your ride?" he asked, his voice matching his incredulous look.

"Doesn't look like a pimp, does he?" Rachel said.

"It's a loaner," I said.

"From who?"

"My dad."

He looked even more confused.

"You and Wanda work together?" I asked.

He nodded.

Soft spoken and easy going, he was as much as six inches taller than my six feet. His dark skin shined even in the dim light from the street lamp above us, and I couldn't tell if its sheen was the result of oil, sweat, or the thick humidity of the moist night air.

"You know her family?"

"Daughter teaches here," he said. "Son's in prison."

"They racist?"

"Miss Wanda's not," he said

"What about Michael?"

He shrugged. "'Bout like most people 'round here. He kill that brother on the river?"

"You think he could?" I asked.

Brow furrowed, eyes narrowed, he cocked his head to the side and considered me. "Most men could kill, but it'd take a bastard and a half to do something like that."

"Could he?"

"Can't say he couldn't," he said. "Don't seem like the type. But hell, most of 'em don't, do they?"

I get most depressed when I'm lying alone in the dark, tossing and turning in my uncomfortable bed, unable to sleep. My little life closes in on me and I feel the full weight of the futility I'm only vaguely aware of most other times.

It happened later that night in my dark bedroom, as lightening from an approaching rainstorm intermittently, momentarily blinded me as it shot through the windows and lit up the small room. The brilliant light was followed by a low rolling thunder in the distance.

It was times like these, when the darkness descended, that I relived my failures, mistakes, and regrets in obsessive detail, wondering what I might have done differently, wishing I could take back so many decisions, imagining where the path not taken would've led.

I never felt more alone or lonely than I did in moments like this. Thinking about all the ways I had managed to alienate others, isolate myself, all the choices away from instead of toward friends, family, and lovers. Why did I need so much space? It was a slow suicide, a potentially fatal flaw I still didn't fully understand.

Anna's pregnant, I thought. Mom's dying. I'm utterly and completely alone.

This nearly always happened when I laid in bed for too long unable to fall asleep or when I fell asleep only to wake a little while later. I felt myself being pulled down—not into the underworld of dreams and rest but into a deep abyss of darkness and despair.

Everybody saw through me. No wonder I was all alone. I deserved to be. I was every bad thing anyone had ever thought I was, and so much they were unaware of. I was a phony, a fake, a hollow, shallow person. Nothing meant anything. Nothing mattered—and what if it did? Was God something I created to give me a sense of purpose, some sort of order to the chaos, some semblance of meaning to the madness.

Even as I felt the emptiness, I knew it wouldn't last. I knew I would feel differently in the morning, but so deep was my sense of futility that I couldn't help but believe that what I was experiencing now was reality, the rest of the time a carefully constructed facade to help me get through the day.

Eventually the first few raindrops pelted the thin glass panes of my windows and pinged off the tin roof, followed by a downpour that brought release, relief, and finally sleep.

I hadn't been asleep long when the first call came.

"You the one asking about Mike?"

The hoarse, twangy female voice was coarse in a way only alcohol, cigarettes, and hard rural living could make it.

"Who?"

"Mike. Mikey. Michael Jensen."

"Yeah. Who's this?"

"Someone who knows."

"Knows what?"

"What he's capable of."

"What's that?"

"Just 'cause a man goes to prison for one thing don't

mean he don't do other, worser things."

"Like what?"

"Ain't gittin' into 'pecifics. Just sayin' don't believe he ain't dangerous. I was with him. I know. I know firsthand what he's like."

"Did he hit you?"

"No," she said. "He beat the shit out of me."

"Did he rape you?"

"Ain't rape when it's your wife. Least that's what he used to say. Shit. I didn't mean to , . . Fuck . . . I've said too much."

She hung up.

The second call came a few minutes later.

Chapter Twenty-six

After being sent home from the hospital to die over six months ago, Mom had lived much longer than anyone imagined she would.

Now she was being put back in the hospital.

Jake had called and asked me to meet him there. As much as he wanted to be with Mom, he hated hospitals and was extremely uncomfortable in situations like this. I could hear both sadness and fear in his voice and told him I'd get there as fast as I could.

Suddenly my self-pity and sadness seemed silly and self-indulgent. I could lose my mom tonight. As I sped toward Bay Medical Center in Panama City, I couldn't think of anything else—not the finality of Anna's pregnancy, not the lynching of a black man who was already dead and my best friend's reaction to it, not the escape of an inmate or his mother's concern about him, not the new chaplain who'd soon have my job, and not the serial rapist branding his victims with a knife.

As much as those things mattered to me, they didn't mean anything at the moment.

Though I was here strictly as a son, I parked in one of the places reserved for clergy because it was closest and quickest and not being used in the middle of the night.

I found Dad and Jake talking with the doctor outside her door. He was a short, fat man with thick, longish, curly black hair and glasses.

"I was just telling your father and brother that your mom's suffering from bleeding esophgeal varices."

"Her throat's bleeding," Jake said.

"We'll treat it with endoscopic sclerotherapy," the doctor said, "but if we can't get it under control . . ."

He drifted off and let that hang there a moment. None of us spoke into the vacuous void.

The truth is," he said, "she's already lived longer than we thought she would. She may just surprise us again."

"What she needs is a transplant," Jake said.

The doctor nodded. "A liver transplant would be a highly effective treatment," he said, pushing his glasses up on his nose. "And who knows, we may still get one. Does she have at least six months sobriety?"

We all looked at each other.

"I think so," I said, nodding. "There haven't been any signs. And I'd know them."

"He's a drunk too," Jake said to the doctor, nodding toward me, and I could detect no malice in his voice. "She ain't been drinkin'."

"Well let's hope for the best," he said.

"Is there anything we can do to help her chances of getting a transplant?" I asked.

He shook his head. "All we can do is wait."

Jake sighed and turned and walked into Mom's room.

"Thank you," I said, and Dad and I followed after Jake.

Mom was sleeping in a nearly upright position, her mouth open, distressed gurgling and snoring sounds coming from it. Her jaundiced skin looked as thin and taut as parchment, etched by fine lines and small wrinkles.

"God I can't stand to see her like this," Jake said.

Dad nodded.

"She's gonna be okay," Jake said. "All she's got to do is hang on until we get her a transplant. And she will. She's strong."

Convinced more than ever that Mom had been holding on because Jake was unable to let her go, I started to say something to him, but knew he would never hear it. Besides, how could I encourage him to let our mother die?

Mom's lids parted and she looked up at us with weak, sallow eyes.

She seemed to be taking her final breaths, her helplessness increased by her inability to speak.

"We're here, Mama," Jake said, as only a Southern boy could. "We're right here." Without meaning to, Jake sounded patronizing.

She gave a half-smile half-frown expression that made my eyes sting and moisten.

"We're gonna get you a transplant, Mama," Jake said, his voice cracking slightly as his eyes filled with tears. "I swear to God we are."

Her lids closed and she fell back asleep.

We were quiet for a long while, but eventually, inevitably our talk turned to the case.

"I think he was messin' around with some white woman," Jake said, "and her husband decided to teach him a lesson."

I shook my head in disbelief. "You think he learned it?" I asked, an angry edge of sarcasm in my voice.

"I'm just sayin' that's the most likely thing that happened. It could be your inmate, but then why string him up?"

Ignoring Jake, I turned to Dad. "I think we're spending too much time looking in the woods," I said. "If he's still in the area, he's probably holed up on a houseboat or in one of the camps, waiting for things to die down so he can slip out—probably on a boat. He could head either direction on the river, come out at any town along the way, and disappear."

Dad nodded. "I'll have them start searching the camps and houseboats in the morning."

"Rachel Mills said they found water in the victim's lungs," I said.

"Yeah," he said. "But they don't think drowning is the cause of death."

"But at some point he was in the water," I said.

We grew silent, our gazes drifting back to Mom.

"We need to get someone to stay with her," Dad said.

"I've got somewhere I have to be," Jake said.

"I'll stay," I said.

"But for how long?" Dad asked. "You two can't do it alone. We'll have to hire someone. Have either of you called Nancy?"

"I ain't callin' her," Jake said.

"I've tried. I'll call her again in the morning and let her know," I said.

"Why?" Jake asked. "She don't care."

Eventually they left, and Mom and I were alone. Pulling one of the cushioned chairs over beside her bed, I sat down. Resting my elbow on the arm of the chair, and my head in my hand, I tried unsuccessfully to get to sleep.

After a short while of being unable to sleep I decided to call Nancy.

Divorcing herself from the chaos that was our family, my older sister Nancy had moved to New York the day after graduating from high school. Since then she'd had the least amount of interaction with us she could. None with Jake.

When after several rings I got her voicemail. I looked at my watch. It was a little after three here, an hour later in New York.

"It's John," I said softly. "Mom's been put back in the hospital. I'm sure she'd love to see you. If you want to see her don't wait. Call me when you can."

I gave her the number and clicked off.

The call back was almost immediate.

"I can't deal with this right now, John," she said.

"Let me know when it'd be more convenient for you. I'll see what I can do," I said with an edge in my voice reserved only for family.

She hung up on me.

I leaned my head back and rubbed my eyes and I could feel the tension in my neck and shoulders, the fatigue in my stinging eyes.

A few minutes later, my phone rang again.

"It's me," she said.

"We don't have a choice about when we deal with this," I said. "Just how."

"I know. I'm sorry. Let's start over."

"Okay. Nancy this is John. Mom's been put in the hospital and isn't doing very well."

"Oh, John, I'm so sorry to hear that," she said. "How long does she have?"

"I'm not sure," I said, "but if she doesn't receive a transplant, not long."

She was silent a long time.

"You going to come?" I asked.

She sighed heavily into the phone and I had to hold it away from my ear for a moment. "I guess," she said.

"Before or after she dies?" I asked.

"Really not sure," she said. "When I decide, you'll be the first to know."

Chapter Twenty-seven

I was in the chapel Monday morning counseling with Sandy Hartman when the second body was discovered.

The more Sandy spoke the more splotchy his face became, and though his voice was soft, his words carefully chosen, real anger and pain leaked out of them.

"I've never felt so helpless in my life," he was saying. "I tried to fight. I tried to get away. I tried everything I could. Nothing worked. He was so strong. So powerful. Like he had this force coming from within him."

As I listened, I saw Chaplain Singer through the narrow panel of glass in my door. He stood there for a moment, then, with a look of frustration, motioned me over.

I shook my head and nodded toward Sandy, but his expression grew more intense and he continued to motion for me.

I had spent the weekend with Mom in the hospital. Mostly sleeping and unable to speak when she was awake, the quiet gave me extended time to think, to process the things swirling around my mind. Our attempts at communicating were more frustrating than anything else, so my weekend was largely wordless.

My aunt Amy had been late relieving me at the hospital and I had been late for work. Chaplain Singer was very disappointed. He had looked at his watch and shook his head when I came in, but continued to whisper into his phone. I knew this was coming, but I had no idea he would interrupt a counseling session to do it.

"I heard you used to drink," he said.

I had opened the door just a few inches and he was leaning forward talking through the narrow opening.

"I'm with someone right now," I said. "I'll talk with you when we're finished."

"You're not hungover, are you?"

I shook my head.

The question's only purpose was provocation. He seemed frustrated it didn't provoke me.

We were quiet a moment.

"Warden Matson runs a very tight ship," he said. "It's his way or the highway. If you don't get on board, you're gonna get run over."

If he used one more ra-ra cliché I might just have to step out into the hall and pummel him.

"You're already on his bad side," he said. "You better tread carefully."

I held my hand up. "Uncle," I said. "I can't take any more."

He looked confused, then shook his head. "I don't know if I've met anybody quite as self-destructive as you."

"Then you really need to get out more."

I closed the door and apologized to Sandy. As I walked past him, I glanced down at the scar on his neck. From this angle I could see it better, and I realized it wasn't just a straight line, but looked to be more complex.

"That little fucker has a real hard-on for you, doesn't he?" Sandy said.

I had never heard him talk like that before, and I wondered if it was a result of the rape.

"Not me so much as my job."

"You're not going anywhere, are you?" he asked, his

voice quiet again and slightly panicked below the surface.

I shook my head.

"You don't know how much this is helping," he said. "If we had to stop . . . I'm not sure what I'd do."

"We won't stop," I said.

He nodded and gave me a small, tight-lipped smile.

We were quiet a moment and he began to relax again.

"You mind if I take a better look at your neck?" I asked. "Your collar covers part of it, and I still haven't gotten a good look at the scar."

He turned his head and pulled back the light brown collar of his correctional officer uniform.

I stood, walked around my desk, and leaned over to get a better look.

It wasn't just a cut, but a mark, a symbol of some sort. I was sure of it now. Whatever the symbol, it was significant to the rapist, and could very well be the key to catching him.

The shank being used to inflict the wound had to be extremely sharp, almost like a scalpel. The scar consisted of a vertical line with a smaller horizontal line intersecting three-quarters of the way up on one end and two smaller lines at the other end extending out at a forty-five degree angle. This made it look like a cross on one end and an arrow on the other.

"Do you know what it stands for?" he asked.

I shrugged. "Let me look into it and see what I can find out."

"Thanks," he said.

Before I could say anything else, the phone on my desk rang.

"Chaplain Jordan," I said.

"John," Jake said. "We've got another one."

"Another what?" I asked.

"Body," he said. "On the river. You're not gonna believe this one. Dad said meet him at Turtle Mason's houseboat."

Chapter Twenty-eight

Turtle Mason, also known as Snake Man Mason and Barefoot Mason, lived in a battered old houseboat on the Apalachicola River.

The quintessential river rat, Turtle lived a primitive life in the hardest way possible, and seemed at least twice as old as his sixty-something years. Subsisting on cheap beer, homemade hooch, and the creatures he pulled from the river and swamp, Turtle caught snakes, turtles, and the occasional gator and sold them to a wholesaler who came to the end of the road to meet him every three weeks.

A local legend, stories about Turtle had grown to mythic proportions over the years. He was missing teeth from inebriated brawls, toes from river rot, and chunks of calf muscle from gator bites. Whether on the hot pavement of town or deep in the snake-filled swamp, Turtle Mason never wore shoes.

By the time Sandy and I had launched his boat at the end of the road, Rachel had arrived and we pulled up to the dock to pick her up. The day was bright and hot but the wind that whipped the faded flag at the landing helped and held the promise of rain.

"Whatta we got?" she asked.

I shrugged. "No idea but I can imagine."

"Crime scene unit's on the way," she said.

I shook my head. If something had happened to Turtle

Mason, the entire community would mourn—including me.

Turtle and I had never been close. We were from different cultures. Unlike most of the kids I had grown up with, the river had never been a big part of my life. The river rat subculture was one of fishing, hunting, boating, skiing, tubing, and just hanging out on a sandbar—all in various stages of intoxication. Underage drinking and over-the-limit fishing and hunting weren't activities the sheriff's son was often invited to. But Turtle's legend extended far beyond the banks of the river.

Sandy gunned the motor, the bow of the boat coming up out of the water as we sped away from the landing. Expertly navigating us toward Turtle's place, Sandy carefully negotiated the boat around branches floating down the river, fallen trees sticking up out of the water, and sandbars created by river bottom dredging done by the Corp of Engineers.

As we raced past the thick green growth of the river swamps starting at the banks and stretching back for unseen miles, I wondered if Michael Jensen was hidden among them watching us. I had the same thought when we passed the dilapidated old camps spread sporadically along the embankments or the many houseboats moored to the cypress trees they held.

When we arrived, hair windblown, eyes watery, we found Dad, two of his deputies—one of them Jake, Fred Goodwin, and Robert Pridgeon, his gray-and-green game warden's uniform soaked through. Dad was standing in the small deck of Turtle's houseboat. The others were seated in their boats, which were tied to Turtle's.

The homemade houseboat was a patchwork quilt of found materials, none of which matched. Under a rusted and dented tin roof, the small one-room floating shack was formed from cypress and pine planks, oak lumber, plywood, polyurethane, insulation, and old road signs.

"This little place is gonna get real crowded in a few

minutes," Dad said. "I'd like for you and Rachel to take a look at it together before it does."

"Whatta we got?" Rachel asked.

Dad shook his head. "Wouldn't know how to tell you. Wouldn't want to if I did. You'll have to look for yourself. Just be ready. It's bad."

Rachel and I stepped aboard the small houseboat, which was still rocking slightly from our wake. The tiny covered deck was filled with empty beer cans, fishing gear, and a single low-standing wooden chair.

Inside, assaulted by the smell of death and decay, we found a smoke-saturated single room filled with empty beer cans, several glass aquariums, five-gallon plastic buckets, and croaker sacks. The dark room was damp and dank and you could see the river between the wooden planks forming the floor. In the center of the room a pallet consisting of two green army blankets and a grease and dirt-soiled pillow without a case laid directly on the floor.

Sunlight streaming through the holes in the boards and the spaces between them provided the only illumination in the room.

As my eyes adjusted, I could see that there was movement in several of the croaker sacks, and that the aquariums were full of snakes, turtles, and baby gators.

"Are those sacks moving?" Rachel asked.

"They've got snakes in them," Dad said. "It's how he made his living."

"Snakes?" Rachel said, panic in her voice.

"And they're not all in the croaker sacks or aquariums so watch your step."

Rachel shivered as she looked down around her feet, and I knew how she felt.

"I don't think I can do this," she said.

"I've got a gun," Dad said.

"I do too," she said. "And I still want one of you to carry

me."

"Just a quick look," Dad said, "and then we're out of here and we'll let the crime scene techs deal with 'em."

Rachel nodded without looking up.

As we continued moving forward, a snake slithered out of Turtle's pallet and through two of the floor boards and dropped into the river below, making a loud splash.

"What was that?" Rachel asked.

"Fish jumping," I said.

"God," she said. "I can't remember when I've been so jumpy."

Clinging to us like dew, the dank air left a sticky sheen on our skin and clothes and dampened our hair, and as we drew closer to the back wall, the volume of flies buzzing about us greatly intensified.

Dad stopped abruptly, and Rachel, looking down, walked into him. Stepping around her, I looked up to see Turtle suspended from the back wall of the houseboat.

He was completely naked, the upper half of his body gray, the lower half dark purple. He was held upright by a noose around his neck that looked to be a leather strap of some kind nailed to the wall. Hands at his sides, feet on the floor, disfigured from decay, he looked like something found in a medieval torture chamber.

In front of him on a small picnic table that looked to have been stolen from the state park, was a Victoria's Secret catalog and a large grimy jar of Vaseline.

"Ever seen anything like that?" Dad asked.

We both nodded.

His eyebrows shot up. "Where?"

"Forensics textbook I read recently," I said.

Dad smiled. "My boy the bookworm."

"A training class in Miami," Rachel said.

"Is it what I think it is?" he asked.

"Autoerotic asphyxia," Rachel said. "The noose cuts off

the air when you climax and it makes it more intense. But pass out and you're dead."

Though it was difficult to look at, I studied the body for another moment. The sunken cheeks of Turtle's toothless mouth were covered with gray stubble the color of his long ponytail. Above his dark purple swollen scrotum, his small flaccid penis looked particularly sad and silly.

Unbidden and filled with a sad irony, a line from Hamlet came to mind.

What a piece of work is a man, how noble in reason, how infinite in faculties, in form and moving how express and admirable, in action how like an angel, in apprehension how like a god, the beauty of the world, the paragon of animals.

"So this is probably not Jensen?" Dad said.

"Both victims were hung," Rachel said. "On or near the river."

"Both crimes have a sexual element," I said.

Dad's face formed a question. "This one obviously does," he said. "But the lynching?"

"The killer tied his hands so his genitals would be exposed," I said.

He squinted as he thought about it. "If that was intentional."

"It was," Rachel and I said in unison.

"But this could be accidental, right?" he asked, nodding toward Turtle.

"If it is," I said, "there will be evidence he's done this before. Other paraphernalia."

"Marks on his neck," Rachel added.

That made me think of the rapist at PCI and I felt guilty for not being there right now trying to catch him.

"Though the body's in such bad shape it may be hard to tell," she added.

"One way to find out," Dad said. "Get the snakes out and the lab in. Can you two stick around?"

Rachel nodded.

"I've got to get back to the prison," I said. "I'll check in with you when my shift ends."

"Either of you give me a read on this?" he asked.

We both nodded. "I don't think it's what it appears to be," I said. "It's just a feeling so it means absolutely nothing, but it's what I sense. It's too close in proximity and too similar to the other one. Too many things connect them—the river, the escape, the method—and as different as the circumstances and victims are, they were both found with nooses around their necks."

Chapter Twenty-nine

I had nodded off with a book in my hand when Walker's bark woke me.

It was early evening, the sun still blaring down on the tin can I called home. I had come in after a busy afternoon of counseling inmates and avoiding Chaplain Singer and Warden Matson, changed into shorts and a T-shirt and pulled several books from my shelves.

The books were illustrated guides to signs and symbols. I was trying to identify the mark I had seen on Sandy Hartman's neck. Obviously far more tired than I realized, I had only made it a quarter way through the first book before I dozed off.

When I heard Walker I closed the book dropped it on the pile on the floor next to me, stumbled off the couch, and looked through the window.

My heart rate quickened and my throat constricted when I saw Anna getting out of her car. We hadn't spoken since she told me she was pregnant, and I wasn't ready to talk to her now.

When I opened the door she was squatting next to her car petting Walker. I pushed the door all the way open and sat down in the doorway, my feet on the steps, and waited.

On his way to wellness, Walker had filled out and had most of his hair back. He still barked, jumped, ran around, and wet himself, but he didn't flinch when you tried to pet him.

When Anna stood, Walker immediately began to bark

and jump on her. She squatted back down and pointed at and scolded him. He calmed down and appeared to nod as she talked to him, but when she stood and tried to walk away, he yelped and began pawing her again.

"Any suggestions?" she said to me.

"I think it's good practice," I said. "Children and puppies can't be that different."

She frowned and rolled her eyes.

"He doesn't look like a puppy," she said.

"Trauma from the abuse he suffered stunted his development," I said. "He's a puppy on the inside."

For a long moment she just stood there staring at me, seemingly oblivious to Walker barking and jumping on her, and then she burst into tears.

I jumped up and bounced down the steps, crossing the distance between us in seconds. When I reached her, I grabbed Walker's collar and slung him off her. He yelped and ran off a few feet and began barking and wetting again.

"You just sent his recovery into regression," she said, wiping her eyes and sniffling.

"I don't care," I said. "Are you okay?"

She shook her head.

"What's wrong?"

"What were you doing before I got here?" she asked.

I told her. Everything.

"I want us to go inside and I want to help you look for the symbol in your books," she said.

"Okay."

"I know we have things we need to say," she said, "but I don't want to talk about any of that tonight."

I nodded.

"I've missed you. Need to be with you. I want us to act the way we did before I told you . . . what I did. I need you to be just the same. I can't handle it if you're mad at me."

"I'm not," I said.

I wasn't sure what I was. I felt so much. And it was hard to distinguish between emotions. But I could be whatever she needed me to be tonight. I could forget about Mom, the escape, the murders, the rapes, the world and everything in it. Could even kick Walker if I needed to.

Inside, while I fixed us some sweet tea, she changed out of the dress Walker had muddied, borrowing a pair of sweat pants and a Florida State T-shirt. Finishing the drinks before she had changed and freshened up, I began picking up around the trailer—putting empty Dr. Pepper cans in the recycle bin, a scattered dish or two in the sink, and a few magazines and newspapers in the trash.

When she rejoined me we sat on the couch beside each other in silence for a few moments drinking our tea.

After a while she said, "Thank you."

I smiled at her.

"I'm gonna break my own rule," she said, "and say one thing about my, ah, situation, and then we'll speak of it no more."

"They're your rules," I said.

"I didn't mean for this to happen," she said. "Took all precautions."

"Then it must be fate," I said.

"I'm gonna let that little comment slide for now because I don't want to get into it," she said, "but don't push it. So what are we looking for?"

I drew the symbol I had seen on Sandy Hartman's neck on the back of an envelope I was using for a bookmark. It looked like a short sideways cross with an arrow on the end.

"I've seen that before," she said.

"I thought the same thing."

We each took a book from the stack and began flipping through them.

Sitting so close to Anna again, I could feel my desire rising, my hurt and anger and disappointment dissipating.

She'd never been mine. But until now there had been a chance. Slim, but existent. Now there was none.

Anna sat with her legs folded beneath her, the tops of her tanned toes exposed. Seeing the way the soft fabric of the sweat pants and T-shirt fit her soon-to-be transformed body made it difficult to concentrate, and the fragrance drifting over me every time she moved or tossed her hair, subtle and tinged with a hint of sweetness, didn't help.

I pictured her naked, as I often did, but this time with the heightened beauty the blush of pregnancy brings—smooth, rounded belly, arched back, full breasts, maternal glow.

"Do you think all his victims have the same mark Sandy does?"

"DeLisa Lopez was supposed to make some discrete inquiries about that this afternoon," I said. "My guess is they do."

She nodded without looking up, her gaze trained on the book in her lap.

I looked back down at mine, and we were silent for a few minutes.

"This it?" she asked.

Chapter Thirty

"It's the sign for Sagittarius," she said.

The symbol she was pointing to was similar but not exactly like the one carved into Sandy's neck. The proportions were different, and it was longer.

"An astrological sign," I said. "That's original."

"Says it's the sign of the archer," she said. "In Greek mythology when Cronus was trying to seduce Philyra, he hid from his jealous wife in the form of a stallion. Then a child was born that was half man and half horse—a centaur."

I studied the symbol a little longer, trying to recall what I had seen earlier in the day.

"Could this be it?" she asked. "The arrow could be phallic. Maybe he thinks he's a stud or hung like a horse."

I shrugged. "Maybe, but we better keep looking—and I'm not just saying that because I don't want you to leave."

She smiled. "Oh I know. You're just thorough."

"I really am," I said. "This could take all night."

She smiled again, and I thought if pregnancy made her any more radiant I wasn't sure if I could be restrained.

"We do what we must for justice," she said.

We returned to our respective searches and a few minutes later Walker announced the arrival of DeLisa Lopez.

When Lisa saw what we were doing, she frowned. "You told her?"

I nodded. "I tell her everything."

"But—"

"I'm his Flambeau when Merrill's not around," Anna said.

"His what?"

"Flambeau to his Father Brown."

Lisa narrowed her eyes and furrowed her brow in confusion.

"I'm his sometime Watson," Anna explained.

When Lisa still seemed lost, I said, "She assists me in investigations, but even if she didn't, I tell her everything."

"But this is so—"

"I'm the very soul of discretion," Anna said.

"It's okay," I said. "What'd you find out?"

She hesitated a minute, then sighed heavily. "They all have it."

"This?" I asked, holding up the drawing I had made for Anna.

She nodded.

"All of them?" Anna asked.

Lisa hesitated again, but not as long this time. "All the ones I talked to."

"Any idea what it is?" Anna asked.

Lisa shook her head.

"Wanna help us look?" Anna said.

"Do I get sweat pants and sweet tea too?" she asked.

While I fixed Lisa a glass of iced tea Anna showed her the Sagittarius sign. I just assumed she was kidding about the sweat pants.

Perhaps because of fatigue but more likely because she was in such close proximity to Anna, Lisa didn't look nearly as sultry tonight. Her skin and hair and eyes were just as exotic, just as suited for South Florida summer nights, every bit as out of place in an old North Florida house trailer, but somehow they just weren't as sensuous, weren't as spicy.

"That could be it," Lisa said. "I don't know."

She was sitting on the floor, looking at the book on the coffee table.

When I set the glass down beside the book, she said, "Do you have a coaster?"

I shook my head. "It's not that kind of joint."

She took a closer look at the wobbly, marred table and nodded.

"Just keep it off the books and no one will get hurt," Anna said.

I laughed.

For the next fifteen minutes or so we all sipped tea and flipped pages, pretty much in silence, and then I saw two symbols that if joined could actually be what we were looking for.

"Look at this," I said, holding up the book so they could see.

The page showed the standard male and female gender signs derived from Mars and Venus.

"If you drop the circles and combine them," I said, holding up my drawing, "isn't this what you'd get?"

They both studied the page then began to nod.

"Or something very close to it," Lisa said.

"It'd account for the sexual component," Anna said.

"It's like he's making his own transgender sign," I said, flipping the page to see if the book showed any.

The transgender sign shown was a male with a stroke.

"That's it," Anna said. "Has to be. He's making his own sign but it's too similar to that not to mean something like it."

"He might be trying to express sexual confusion by combining the two," Lisa said. "Especially when coupled with what he makes them do—the whole self-sodomy thing. He doesn't know if he's Mars or Venus. Or maybe he's trying to become both simultaneously. Making his victims do the same."

"Forced oneness?" Anna said.

"Or androgyny," Lisa said.

"If we're right," I said, "what does it tell us about him?"

"Probably not your typical rapist," Lisa said. "The act may be less about rage than sexual confusion and control. I'm not saying there's not real anger, even rage. Just that it might be more about experimentation. Like maybe he's exploring his own sexual confusion with real live dolls."

Chapter Thirty-one

Driving to work the next morning I thought about all that was going on. There seemed to be too much to deal with, and I was having difficulty focusing on anything. As I tried to think about what the rapist's mark meant, I found myself worrying about Mom, wondering if it really was the end this time, and when I tried to concentrate on the lynching or Turtle, I'd drift off into thoughts about Anna being pregnant or how it appeared my time as chaplain of PCI was coming to an end.

My thoughts continued to circle relentlessly and I wondered if this was how it felt to have attention deficit disorder.

When I neared the turnoff for the prison, I met Dad going the opposite way. He hit his lights and pulled off the road. I slowed, circled around, and pulled up behind him. A clean cut thirty-something white man in a black suit, white shirt, and black tie sat in his passenger seat.

Dad got out and met me between our vehicles. His passenger stayed in the car.

"I'm gonna go out on a limb here and say he's some sort of fed," I said.

"Can't campaign, for all the damn babysitting I'm having to do," he said. "He's secret service. Someone got a counterfeit bill at a bar on the beach and as a courtesy I've got to drive him down there and back and waste half my day."

I nodded.

"Have you had a chance to talk to Merrill yet?" he asked.

I shook my head. "Not yet but I will."

He nodded and frowned. "Primary's less than a week away," he said. "Hell, I may not even make it into the general election."

"It's that close?"

"One of the professors at the college did a poll," he said.

As the prison personnel passed by on their way to work, Dad waved and smiled. A few waved back. Most didn't even look in our direction.

"Have you found out anything about that Marianna minister Merrill saw get lynched?" I asked.

He frowned again, nodded very slowly, and let out a long sigh. "There was a Deacon R. L. Jenkins who went missing back then. Some church money vanished too and everyone assumed he stole it and took off with his girlfriend."

"She go missing too?"

"I'm just telling you what the rumor was," he said. "The good reverend was married with four kids. Folks always suspected he had a girlfriend and that she lived here, and they assumed she was the reason he stole the money. It's all just gossip."

"Except he really went missing. Never showed up again."

"He could just be across the country scamming some other congregation," he said.

"Could be but we both know he's not."

"Listen," he said. "This has to stay very quiet until after the election. If this comes out . . . This thing's been layin' around for nearly thirty years. Let's leave it alone for a few more months."

I didn't say anything.

"I know what you're thinking," he said, "but if I lose

the election, I won't be able to do anything about it—won't be able to do anybody any good, and neither will you. A different sheriff's not gonna let you be involved in his cases."

"I don't know," I said. "Fred Goodwin said if he wins he's gonna ask me to be his lead investigator."

"I've asked you to come work for me a hundred times," he said. "Are you—"

"I'm just telling you what he said. Not looking for a job."

I heard a horn honk behind me and I turned to see Chaplain Singer pulling up and rolling down his window.

"Warden wants to see us first thing," he said. "Wouldn't be late if I was you."

Chapter Thirty-two

The new warden's office was as different as it could be and still have the same carpet, wall-color, and furniture. Gone was Edward Stone's framed crayon-colored drawing his son had made just before he died. Gone were his degrees and Florida Department of Corrections citations. Replacing them were framed photographs of inmates working on the Angola farm, Louisiana Department of Corrections citations, and religious and motivational posters of sentimental images and clichéd sayings.

LSU memorabilia, including a football signed by the team and coaching staff, lined the bookshelves between DOC manuals, religious and law enforcement books, and a handful of Gideon Bibles.

When I had arrived, Bat Matson was drinking coffee from a Styrofoam cup and talking with the colonel, the major, the shift OIC, the inspector, and Chaplain Singer.

"You boys 'scuse me a minute," he said. "It's come-to-Jesus time for the chaplain."

My heart was pounding and I felt angry and embarrassed, and I was disappointed in how I was handling this—especially my ego response to being humiliated in front of the security staff and the man who was supposed to be my assistant.

As the security staff walked out, none of them spoke or

even looked at me.

The colonel closed the door, and only Matson, Singer, and I were left in the room.

"Have a seat," Matson said.

I sat beside Singer in one of the chairs across from Matson's desk.

"Chaplain," Matson said, "I'm not sure what kind of asylum Warden Stone ran, and I know a real well-run institution takes some getting used to—especially by the more free thinkers on staff, but I've made it clear what I expect."

He paused, but I didn't say anything.

"Do you have anything to say?" he asked.

I shook my head.

"Chaplain, I think you have real potential," he said.

Beside me Singer nodded.

"You seem to be pretty popular with the staff and the inmates. And you seem to like being a chaplain."

I nodded.

"Just not enough to do what I tell you and stop playing detective."

I didn't respond. He was obviously going somewhere with this and I decide just to let him get there on his own.

"After repeated verbal warnings," he said, "you have continued to neglect your chaplaincy duties. I have no choice but to place a written reprimand in your personnel file."

There were few things more difficult than firing a state employee. Only teachers on continuing contract had more job security. He couldn't just fire me, but he could make me so miserable I left on my own, all the while establishing a written record justifying a dismissal if I didn't.

"What exactly am I receiving a reprimand for?" I asked.

"Dereliction of duty," he said.

I shook my head. "You might be able to argue I do more than what's in my job description," I said, "but no one can say I do less."

"This other stuff you're doing—the stuff I specifically told you not to do—is taking time away from your ministry."

"Give me one example," I said.

Matson looked at Singer. Singer said, "You came in late yesterday and left early."

"And the reason I was able to do that," I said, "is because of all the comp time I have from all the overtime I've worked. Plus I came back in yesterday and worked late."

"I didn't realize—" Singer began.

"That's because you weren't here," I said.

His face turned red and he looked at the warden.

"I gave him the afternoon off to finish moving and unpacking," Matson said.

"Do you have any idea how many inmates I counseled with yesterday?" I asked.

Neither man said anything.

"Do you know that I've been without a staff chaplain assistant for two years, and in that time I haven't missed a single service or death notification? Did you know that a survey done by the lead chaplain showed that more programs for more religions were taking place in the PCI chapel than any other chapel in the state?"

Both men seemed to be searching for something to say.

"I know you want him to be the senior chaplain here," I said. "And I know you don't want me involved in criminal investigations inside or outside the prison, but to accuse me of not doing my job . . . Let me see if I can put it in a way that you Louisiana boys will understand. That dog just won't hunt."

Chapter Thirty-three

"**I** live in constant fear," Sandy Hartman was saying. "I'm not sleeping well. Have nightmares when I do."

We were in my office in the midst of one of our impromptu counseling sessions.

To my left a light smattering of raindrops from an approaching thunderstorm speckled the window.

"I can't stand to be alone, but that's how I spend most of my time," he continued. "I'm always looking over my shoulder—especially out here. I get physically sick every time I get anywhere close to the medical building."

The light coming through my window dimmed as the clouds rolled in and thunder rolled in the distance.

"I just keep thinking he's going to do it again," he said. "He seems so strong, so powerful—not even human—like he can do whatever he wants to me anytime he wants to, and there's not a damn thing I can do about it."

I nodded, but didn't say anything.

His face was hard, etched with anguish and anger, and his sunken eyes had dark circles around them.

"Do you think a man can be more than a man?" he asked. "Superhuman somehow. Filled with a power that . . . I don't know . . . makes him invisible? Invincible?"

"Do you?" I asked.

He didn't answer right away. Turning toward the window, he seemed to stare at the approaching storm.

"I used not to," he said, still staring out the window, his voice barely audible.

The darkening day made my office seem far brighter, the harsh overhead light accentuating the pale, taut skin of Sandy's face and the bruise-like bags beneath his hollow eyes.

"Now I'm not so sure," he said.

"He's not invincible or inhuman," I said. "We're going to catch him."

"We?" he asked. "You didn't tell the—"

"DeLisa Lopez," I said. "She's the one who brought him to my attention in the first place. She's going through the medical logs and duty rosters right now to narrow down our field of suspects."

"Does she know about me?"

I shook my head.

He looked relieved.

"I haven't told anyone and I won't," I said.

He nodded slowly then fell silent for a long moment.

After a while he said, "I want to help y'all catch him."

I paused for a moment before saying, "I'm not sure that's such a good idea."

"It's not about vengeance or anything like that," he said. "You know I'm not that kind of person. I just want to help stop him from hurting anyone else."

"I don't know," I said.

I couldn't imagine he'd be much help and there was a chance he'd get in the way or wind up being more traumatized, but if there was a chance it might empower him, might help him take back his life, it might just be worth the risk.

"Please."

"If you do Ms. Lopez will probably guess why."

He nodded. "It's okay. I just really need to do this, to help in some way, to face my fear, stand up like a man and to quit feeling like a victim."

Chapter Thirty-four

"We've got some likely candidates," Lisa said, "but there're so many it's overwhelming."

Sandy and I had joined Lisa in her office inside the medical building and were now seated across her desk going over possible suspects in the rape case.

"Here's a list of possibles," she said, handing me a sheet of paper with two columns of names on it.

She hesitated before handing Sandy one. "Are you sure you want to do this?"

He nodded and held out his hand.

She handed him a copy of the list. "Do you know how we arrived at this list?"

He shook his head.

"What John asked me to do was take the . . . ah, attacks that we know about, the logs from the officer's desk in the waiting room, the duty rosters, and the control room logs and cross-reference them. Anyone—staff, officer, or inmate—who was in or around the building at the time of all the attacks we know of made the list."

"This is a lot of names," Sandy said.

She frowned and nodded, then looking at me said, "This doesn't include all the women like me who work in the building—nurses, classification officers, secretaries."

"It's not a woman," Sandy said.

His voice was tight and a little shaky, which matched the rest of him. From the moment we walked into the medical building, a visible change had come over him. Tremors were running the length of his body, his eyes darted around, and he was continually looking over his shoulder.

She looked at him then back at me when he looked down at the list again.

I nodded.

"Okay," she said. "I'm glad I left them off."

We were all silent a moment, looking at the list.

"How do we even start to narrow it down?" Sandy asked.

"We have records for all the inmates," I said. "If they're in for rape, they stay on the list automatically. For the rest let's look at what they're in for and see who we can mark off. As far as staff, the ones we know the best and suspect the least we'll move to the bottom of the list and see what we're left with."

"We're still gonna be left with a lot," Lisa said, "and we can't be absolutely certain that he's even on here. What if he slipped in and out without being seen?"

I shrugged. "All we can do is work with what we have. It's as good a place to start as any."

"Then let's get started," Sandy said. "The sooner we get this prick the better."

I looked back at the list and began to draw a pencil line through the names of officers and staff we didn't need to waste time on.

"I see that I made the list," I said.

She nodded. "You spend a lot of time in Classification," she said with a smile. "Or you used to. Though a couple of times you were in Confinement. Since one of the attacks occurred between Confinement and Medical I included everyone in Confinement during all the attacks."

"Not the inmates in cells?" Sandy asked.

She shook her head.

"Do you object to me crossing my name off the list?" I asked.

She smiled and shook her head.

"Am I on here as a victim or a suspect?" Sandy asked.

"I'm sorry," Lisa said. "I wasn't even thinking. I'll need to take the other victims off before we go any further. Give me those and let me redo the list."

She held out her hand.

"We've looked at these a good bit already," I said. "If you take them off now, chances are we'll notice that they're missing. The only way to ensure their anonymity is to just leave them on."

"You're right," she said. "I'm sorry. I should've thought about that before. I was just in such a hurry."

"It's fine," I said. "Don't worry about it. I just appreciate you doing it."

We spent the next hour or so going through the list line by line, examining inmate files, discussing the staff we each knew well. When we were finished, we had narrowed our list to a dozen inmates.

"I really don't think we should exclude staff," Sandy said. "I see a few names on here—like Shane—that . . . I don't know. I just think we need to look real hard at staff too."

"We will," I said. "But we've got to start somewhere. And since he uses a shank . . ."

He nodded. "So of these who do we start with?"

I glanced at the list again.

"Ronnie Taunton," I said.

Chapter Thirty-five

Ronnie Taunton, an inmate orderly assigned to Medical, was a stocky white man of a little over five and a half feet with pale skin and bushy mouse-brown hair. He was quiet in a creepy way. A loner. Intelligent. He was serving time for aggravated assault, but on more than one occasion had been accused, arrested for, but never convicted of, rape.

His white meant-to-be-loose inmate uniform was stretched tightly over the large frame of his muscular body. His smile, on the rare occasion he flashed it, was wolfish, and if the dull eyes behind his big black glasses were windows to his soul, he either didn't have one or the one he had was as vacuous as dark matter in a black hole.

I found him mopping the back hallway of Medical outside the infirmary. I had come alone. Lisa has suggested that I might get more out of him this way, and there was no way I was going to let Sandy interview someone who might possibly be the monster who had scarred him for the rest of his life.

"How's it going?" I asked.

He stopped mopping and raised up.

"Hey, Chaplain," he said. "How are you?"

"Good," I said. "You?"

He shrugged.

Expecting me to pass by like I normally did, he began to mop again, but stopped when he noticed I was still standing there.

The tile floor gleamed—even in the dull, greenish light of the Fluorescents overhead—and didn't appear to need cleaning.

"You down here playing detective?" he asked.

"Why do you say that?"

"You got the look," he said. "You always speak, and if any of us got something to say, you'll stop and listen to us, but when you stop on your own . . ."

I nodded. "Pretty perceptive," I said. "Sounds like you've thought about it."

"What else I got to do?"

With his green-and-black prison tats, his hospital-pale skin, and his thick, big-framed glasses, Ronnie Taunton looked like a rapist, and I was trying not to let that have too big an impact on my impression of him.

It wasn't easy.

"Some people say talkin' to you's no different from talking to a cop or CO," he said.

I laughed. "Not even close. I have very different priorities, a lot less restrictions, and I just help out occasionally. I'm strictly amateur hour."

Down the hallway not far from where we stood, the suicide cells were empty and dark, their doors slightly ajar, and I wasn't sure if that was a good thing or not.

"You seen or heard anything strange down here?" I asked.

"Like what?"

"Anything."

He shrugged. "Always something strange goin' on. I just try to keep my head down and do my time so I can get out."

"How much longer you got?"

"Couple a years."

"What're you in for?" I asked.

"A misunderstanding."

"People usually don't go down for those," I said.

"This one put the other guy in the hospital."

I nodded.

We were quiet a moment.

Through the windows of the left wall, I could see that the rows of beds in the infirmary were empty, their bright white sheets and pillow cases crisp and clean.

The infirmary bathroom, like the inmate bathrooms in the dorms, was open, its entrance and stalls as devoid of doors as the inmates were of privacy. From it came the constant monotonous, watery thump of a leaky shower head dripping onto the tile floor.

He leaned in and said in a low voice, "Listen, Chaplain, I see and hear a lot. It's almost like I'm invisible. But I don't want to say somethin' about somethin' you're not here about, so why don't you just tell me what it is and I'll tell what I know."

"You're a helpful guy, aren't you?" I asked.

He shrugged. "Do what I can. 'Specially for a man of the cloth."

"You religious?" I asked.

"Sure," he said with a half shrug. "As far as it goes."

From the break room at the end of the hallway, I heard a can drink dislodge, roll through the machine, and bang out at the bottom. It sounded like a cue ball hitting a pocket and rolling through a pool-table. After a moment a large African-American nurse in a bright pink uniform strolled slowly out of the room with a Coke and a Snickers.

When she had made it past us and through the door at the other end of the hall, I said, "You familiar with Salvador Dalí's work?"

"Salva-what?" he asked. "She got something to do with something going on down here?"

"What about assaults?" I asked. "You know of any unreported assaults taking place down here?"

"Could you be more specific?" he asked. "All kinds of assaults."

"Have you heard anyone mention the mark of the beast?" I asked.

He smiled his wolfish grin. "That's what you're here about? Some boys being made to butt-fuck themselves? Why didn't you just say so."

"I heard it's a lot more than that," I said.

He shrugged. "That's all I've heard."

"Who'd you hear it from?" I asked.

He shook his head. "Just around. Here and there."

I smiled.

Another inmate orderly emerged from the infirmary bathroom, a bottle of cleaning solution in one hand, a white rag in another. Like the nurse, I had no idea he was even in the vicinity, and I was reminded again of how many places there were to hide in this building.

"What can you tell me?" I asked.

"Guy's very good," he said. "Seems invisible."

"You think he's gay?" I asked.

I knew from his file he had only been accused of raping women and that one of the things he was charged with was a hate crime for assault on a gay couple. If he was the rapist, being reminded his victims were men should trigger him in some way.

"The fuck should I know?"

"Just asking what you think. Why'd it make you so mad?"

"It didn't," he said. "I just don't know why you're asking me all this."

"I was told you were a guy who knew things," I said. "Especially things that happened in Medical."

"I'm not one of these ignorant assholes around here you can flatter into telling you what you want to know," he said.

I nodded. "Anything else you're willing to tell me?"

He smiled. "Sure," he said, "but you won't believe me."

"Try me."

"I know you think I'm the one doing it, but I'm not. You made the faggot comment to try to get me to react, but it didn't work because it isn't me. Got no interest in any part of a man— least of all his anus."

I nodded.

"You believe me?"

I shrugged.

"I can make you," he said.

"Oh yeah? How's that?"

He turned his head and pulled back his collar to reveal the scar on his neck.

"I'm not the beast," he said. "I just bear his mark."

Chapter Thirty-six

Rachel and I were back on the river.

Bouncing between the three cases—the escape, the rapes, and the murders—was difficult, and it kept me from gaining a normal rhythm or much momentum, but there wasn't much I could do about it—especially with my chaplaincy duties and everything I was doing being scrutinized by Matson and Singer. It was as if this entire thing was a complicated offbeat jazz piece. The key was to play it as it arose—not rush it, not drag behind, and to do so I'd have to fight frustration every step of the way. Impatience was the enemy.

Rachel had commandeered a boat from a fellow FDLE agent and was driving us toward Turtle Mason's houseboat a lot faster than she should.

It had rained recently and the leaves shimmered in the afternoon sunlight, beneath them steam rising off the hot earth. The waters of the Apalachicola seemed clearer and greener, resembling more closely the bay and beyond it the Gulf they were flowing toward than the Chattahoochee and Flint rivers they were flowing from.

As we raced down the wide waterway, I took in the radiant river and felt myself begin to relax, the tension and turmoil in my mind and body being released and carried away, as if washed out to sea.

I took in a deep breath, held it, and let it out slowly, surrendering to my surroundings and a more primal way of being.

Without slowing she turned toward Turtle's and cut the engine, the boat rising on its own wake and riding it in.

Beyond the sagging crime scene tape the small porch area held several of the aquariums and croaker sacks from inside.

"They say all the snakes are out," she said.

"Be sure to let me know," I said.

She punched me in the arm. "I brought you for protection."

"Why are we here again?" I asked.

"They're towing it in today."

"Exactly," I said.

"I want one more look before it's moved. No telling what evidence might be lost or destroyed when they do that."

Lifting the crime scene tape and stepping beneath it, we climbed aboard the boat, each of us careful not to step too close to the croaker sacks.

Pulling a small knife from her pocket, she slit the crime scene tape near the handle and pushed the door open with her foot. Pocketing her knife, she withdrew two pairs of latex gloves and a small flashlight.

"You got anything else in there?" I asked, nodding toward her pocket. "Snake-proof boots? First-aid kit?"

She laughed and handed me a pair of gloves.

We snapped on the gloves and she shined the small light inside.

"Oh, that's a big help," I said.

Standing there side by side, I was reminded again of the difference in our height. She was nearly a foot shorter than me but it seemed like more.

"Don't see anything moving," she said.

"And with that light you definitely would."

"Nobody likes a smart ass," she said.

"I've always wondered what it was," I said.

We stood there looking in for another moment.

"We ready to do this?"

"Sure," I said, "but there's no way they got them all."

We slowly edged our way inside, looking closely, stepping carefully, and began our search.

Much of what had filled the room the first time we were here was now gone. Someone had removed a board from the top of the rear wall to let in more light and we could see more than before.

Most of the aquariums were gone, but the board and cinder block shelves that held them remained. Most of the croaker sacks were gone, but a few still littered the uneven plank floor. The smell of stale smoke still tinged the edges of the air, but it wasn't nearly as strong as it had been.

In the back left corner of the room, a stack of plastic milk crates facing outward held Turtle's clothes—faded T-shirts with beer and rock band logos and well-worn blue jeans and cutoffs, the ends frayed. We looked through every crate, but turned up nothing.

"If this were your house," Rachel said, "where would you hide your JOM?"

I turned and looked down at her. "Where'd you hear that expression?" I asked.

"Jack-off material? I have four older brothers. I'm an investigator with the Florida Department of Law Enforcement."

I nodded.

"Plus," she added with a smile, "why would you think I didn't have some of my own hidden in my house? My brothers never went blind from what they did but I might as well have."

"Alanis," I said. "Classic."

She smiled appreciatively. "You know a lot of shit for a

chaplain."

"I'm not just a chaplain," I said. "I'm a human being too."

With the body removed the flies were gone but mosquitos swarmed in and out of the holes in the boards and the spaces between them. Both of us were continually swatting—occasionally slapping ourselves and smearing blood on our cheeks, necks, and hands.

"So back to my question," she said. "Where would you—"

"Where would you?" I asked. "You're the only one present who's admitted to having any."

"You've studied autoerotic asphyxiation," she said. "How many cases of accidental death caused by it involved women?"

"Good point. Somewhere hidden but easy to get to. Of course if it wasn't anything more explicit than a Victoria's Secret catalog, it wouldn't have to be hidden—speaking of which, did the one he was using have a shipping label on it?"

She shook her head. "It had been torn off."

I raised my eyebrows and looked at her.

She nodded. "Suspicious, huh?"

"Any way to trace the catalog without the label?"

She shook her head.

"Anything helpful from the prelim?" I asked.

She shook her head. "Not really. His injuries aren't inconsistent with accidental strangulation."

I nodded and frowned.

"So," she said again, "back to my question."

"Give me a minute to look around," I said. "Did the techs find anything?"

She shook her head.

"What about other possible nooses?"

"Not a single one," she said.

"Why don't you look for them while I look for the other stuff?" I asked.

"What if I pick one up only to find out it's a snake?"

"Apologize and put it down," I said.

We each began our respective searches but always in close proximity to one another.

"Shouldn't we spread out?" I asked.

She shook her head. "The stuff's probably all together. Besides, I know how freaked out you are by this place."

It took a while but we finally found what we were looking for—a small door in the floor beneath one of his homemade shelves. When we opened it, we discovered a plastic container nailed to the bottom of the boat. It held Turtle's valuables—some cash, a few keys, a couple of family photographs, a few documents, and his porn.

Evidently Turtle liked his women big, big breasted, and hairy. He had quite a collection, and if what was in the hidden crate was what did it for him, Victoria held no secret that would.

"The killer underestimated Turtle," she said.

I smiled and nodded.

"Going from material this explicit to an underwear catalog would be like going from actual intercourse back to upstairs outsidesies."

"Upstairs outsidesies?"

She smiled. "And you know what that means," she said.

"Old Turtle was murdered."

Chapter Thirty-seven

The small, sterile room was dim and quiet, only the sounds of Mom's labored breathing and the hum of the air conditioner keeping it from complete silence.

It was late. I was tired. But unable to sleep.

Continuing to be concerned about the state of my spiritual life, I was still making my way through Thomas Moore's *Dark Nights of the Soul* again, hoping that's all this was, and not how I would be fated to live out the rest of my sentence. I was reading about what Moore says are the links between creativity, spirituality, and struggles, and the need the deep soul has for the darker beauty of our existence.

I found his words soothing, his encouragement to give in to this Saturn state comforting, but my mind continued to drift, pulling me back again and again to the recent events I was searching for a brief reprieve from.

Eventually I closed the book and stood up. Rubbing my eyes and stretching, I walked over to the window and looked out.

It was a dark night. Small pools of light beneath street lamps dotting the darkness, illuminating only the limited area directly under them. The hot night's humidity clung to everything, leaving a damp sheen that glistened like early morning's dew-covered grass.

Standing there looking out at the darkness, seeing both it and a faint reflection of myself in the window, I thought about what it would be like not to have a mom.

We weren't close. She hadn't been a big part of my life for a long time. She wasn't someone I relied on in any way, but the thought of not having her was nearly unbearable.

There was no way to know what the loss of her would be like, how it would impact me, the residual and lasting effects it would have on my life. How much would I miss her? How raw would her death leave me, how vulnerable and exposed her utter and complete and final absence?

My eyes began to sting and water, and I blinked and looked down, trying to keep from crying.

A copy of the Panama City paper on the floor caught my eye and I reached down and picked it up. The Local and State section was on top. A story above the fold showed a picture of a plane like the one I thought I saw when Michael Jensen had escaped.

The story told of a banner plane from the beach that had to make an emergency landing in a nearby state park. The Cessna 175, the one that looked nearly identical to the one I saw, lost power and drifted down into an open area, to the surprise of those picnicking in the park. According to a spokesperson for Air Ads Inc., the pilot did exactly what he was supposed to when he lost power—dropped his banner and looked for a safe place to land. No one was injured in the event and after a spare part was located and placed on the plane, it took off from the park and flew back to the private Air Ads Inc. runway.

In the past six years Air Ads Inc. had had a number of close calls, but only two crashes and one fatality. There was nothing mentioned about the plane I had seen, but I decided to take the paper with me and look into it more closely later.

As I placed the folded paper inside my book, Mom opened her eyes and looked up at me. I moved over and stood by her bed, taking her hand in mine and smiling at her.

"Can I get you anything?" I asked.

She turned her head and looked over at the tray beside her bed, then nodded to the pad of paper and pen she had been using to communicate.

I grabbed them and handed them to her.

She wrote: *Where is Jake?*

"I'm not sure," I said. "Why?"

She scribbled out very quickly: *I'm worried about him. He told me they had an organ for me. The next time I woke up he was gone. He hasn't been back since. That's been a few days ago I think. Hard to tell.*

"I'll check on him," I said. "But don't worry. I'm sure he's fine."

We were silent for a long moment, tears filling her eyes. *They don't have a transplant for me do they?*

"Not that I've heard," I said, "but I'll ask again."

Tears began to stream out of the corners of her eyes and pool in her ears.

I took her hand again. "I love you."

She released my hand, and took up her pen again.

She wrote: *I don't want to die.*

I nodded, squeezed her hand, and said, "I know."

We were quiet again, and in a few moments the phone rang. The loud noise in the quiet room was startling and Mom jumped.

I snatched it up and said, "Hello."

"JJ," a heavily accented Southern voice I only vaguely recognized said.

"Yeah?"

"It's Haywood."

Haywood Smiley owned and operated a bar and drive-thru package store on the edge of Pottersville.

"Son, I'm sorry as hell to have to call you at the hospital but I don't know what else to do."

"What is it?" I asked.

"It's Jake," he said. "He's drunk as fuck and bustin' up the place."

Chapter Thirty-eight

By the time I reached Smiley's Lounge and Package, Jake was outside in the parking lot. He was sitting on the tailgate of his truck, the tips of his pointed-toe cowboy boots just barely scraping the asphalt beneath them.

His face was red and puffy from drink, beginning to bruise from fighting. A smear of blood lay just beneath his nose and his upper lip was swollen. His eyes were bloodshot and looked like he'd been crying.

I pulled up in my pimped-out ride and rolled down the window.

He looked at the car and shook his head. "Hell, I thought it was a drive-by."

He may have slurred his words just a little or I may have imagined it. I wasn't sure.

"You ready?" I asked.

"Not until I get my goddamn keys," he said. "And I ain't riding in that."

I knew better than to argue with a drunk so I parked, went in and got his keys, and drove him home in his truck.

We were quiet for a long while, the empty highway stretching out before us, the darkness gathered at the edge of the headlights threatening to overtake them at any moment.

"This is a switch," he said.

Even at my drunken worst he had never been my designated driver, never had to pick me up from any bar anywhere, but I knew what he meant. I was the alcoholic, the weak one who couldn't handle my drink.

"I ain't as drunk as they think," he said. "I can drive."

I still didn't say anything.

"Drunk as I am, could still kick your ass," he said.

Jake's swagger was worse than his swing. He couldn't take me stone cold sober, but I wasn't about to argue with him—or stop the truck and prove the point.

We rode in silence again for a while. Eventually I became aware of him crying.

"How's Mama?" he asked. "You better not tell her I was drinkin' and fightin'."

"She says you told her they found her a transplant," I said.

"I'm gonna get her a new liver," he said.

"Why would you tell her that?" I asked.

"I'm tellin' you," he said. "I'm gonna fuckin' find her one."

He started crying harder, turning his head as if looking out at something in the darkness, sniffling often, and rubbing his short hair down with the palm of his hand.

"God, this is so fucked up," he said.

I nodded. "Yes it is."

"Ain't talkin' to you," he said.

"I never knew you were such a mean drunk," I said.

"There's a lot you don't know. Hell of a lot. You think you know so much. But you don't. I know so much you don't know."

I nodded.

"Mama's gonna be okay you son of a bitch," he said.

I didn't say anything. Just drove.

By the time I reached his place, he was asleep and Merrill, who had come to give me a ride back to my car, and I had to carry him in and put him to bed.

Chapter Thirty-nine

"So why we here?" Merrill asked.

It was later in the week and we were at the landing, launching his Uncle Tyrone's boat into the river.

A gentle breeze blowing off the rippled water made the late afternoon bearable, but the humidity was high, the mosquitos swarming, the atmosphere heavy.

You could smell the impending rain in the river air.

"Because of what's happened," I said.

"Escaped convict, the lynching, and Turtle?" he asked. "Or somethin' else happen I don't know about?"

"Nothin' happens 'round here without you knowing about it," I said.

I pushed the boat back and jumped in. We drifted backward a few feet and he pulled the crank cord and started the motor.

"So what we gonna do?" he said. "And don't say ride around and await developments."

I laughed.

"Your ass was, wasn't it? You forget what a big ass river this is?"

With the motor only idling we slowly made our way out of the launch area and into the main channel of the wide river.

"Everything's happened within a few miles," I said.

"So we just gonna ride around?"

"And await developments," I said.

He shook his head slowly and smiled appreciatively.

"And if nothin' develops?"

"We keep coming back until it does," I said.

"We gotta get you a girlfriend."

He revved the motor and the boat lifted and shot upriver.

We rode past the tall sand hill the Corps of Engineers' dredging had created and around the smaller sandbars formed as the hill was slowly washed back into the water.

Because it was a weekday and bad weather was approaching, we only saw a few other people—a man and his teenage son on Wave Runners, a couple of fishermen calling it a day, and a few people waving to us from the back porches of camps and the front decks of houseboats.

The spot where the river's most recent victim vanished was marked by a white wooden cross on a cypress tree near the water's edge. The boy, Taylor Smith, drinking and swimming with his friends near one of the sandbars, went under and never came back up. Some people say a gator got him, others that all the dredging had formed air pockets beneath the quicksand-like bottom of the river and he got sucked into one. His name had been painted on the cross and fresh flowers placed on the ground around it.

As we neared the spot, we saw the search and rescue boat coming around the bend. Both boats slowed and came up beside each other. Missing a few of their members, today the team consisted of Todd, Shane, and Kenny. Jake and Fred weren't with them. Sandy was still quit.

"Where's that sorry ass brother of yours?" Kenny asked.

As usual he wore no shirt or shoes, his enormous belly hanging down over his faded blue jeans cutoffs.

"Am I my brother's keeper?" I asked.

"He's been acting strange lately," Shane said. "Is it your mom or something else?"

I shrugged.

"He normally doesn't miss this shit for anything," Todd said.

"Training exercises?" I asked.

"Were," Todd said, "but we just got a call that a guy from Dothan with a camp down here is missing. He spends most summers down here alone, so nobody knew he was gone for a while."

"Where's his place?"

"Just around the next bend," Shane said. "We just searched it. The guy's truck is there, but his boat isn't. No sign of foul play."

"And no sign of Jensen either," Todd added. "He's probably long gone on the dude's boat by now."

None of them had yet to acknowledge Merrill, or even look at him, and so far he hadn't said anything.

"Let us know if you see anything," Shane said.

He cranked the motor and they raced away. For a moment we just sat there rocking in their wake, and as we did, I saw somebody in the woods just behind the cross.

I didn't say anything as Merrill cranked the motor and we pulled away from the spot. When we had rounded the sandbar I told him what I had seen and we quickly devised a plan.

Pulling up to the bank without killing the motor, Merrill dropped me off and continued up the river. Hopefully, whoever I had seen, Michael Jensen in all probability, would think we were still heading away from him.

Eventually Merrill was going to circle back and approach him from the front while I came up behind him.

The river swamp was thick and damp and oppressively hot and humid. No wind could penetrate the dense woods, and it trapped the heat in a wet, sauna-like system that was more tropical than anything else in our region. Within a few moments, I was covered in sweat, my clothes soaked through and clinging to me.

Low-growing ferns covered the ground, and I couldn't see where I stepped.

Everything—the trees, the ferns, the leaves on the ground, the ground itself—was damp as if after a heavy rain, and my shoes were soon soaked and mud covered.

I walked about twenty feet inland, then turned in the direction of the cross and the man behind it. I had no idea how long it would take, and since everything in the woods looked the same, I had no way to judge my progress.

Trying to walk quickly but also be alert and not rush up on him before I realized what I was doing, I was constantly scanning the area, carefully looking through the thick foliage.

It was while doing this that I failed to notice the small fallen pine tree in front of me and tripped over it, hitting the ground hard.

I was able to get my hands down in time, preventing my head from taking the brunt of the blow, but my wrists and body paid the price—and I had the breath knocked out of me.

I waited for a moment, trying to get my breath back, then pushed myself up, pain shooting through my wrists and arms.

Then he was on me, pressing me down to the damp ground, large hunting knife at my throat.

Chapter Forty

"Pull down your pants," he said.

"What?" I asked, stalling.

"Pull down your goddamn pants or I'll slit your fuckin' throat," he said.

His voice was gravelly, as if he had been gargling with glass, and his breath smelled almost as bad as his body. He was heavy and strong, his weight and strength pinning me to the damp ground, and no matter what I did, I couldn't get free.

Was Jensen the rapist?

I tried to recall if any rapes had occurred since he escaped. I couldn't be certain, but I didn't think any had.

"You wanna die?"

"Why are you doing this?" I asked.

"Do what I tell you or I'll kill you," he said.

The knife was large and sharp, and I wondered where he got it. Had he taken it from an empty camp or houseboat, or had he killed for it? Did it belong to Turtle or the man who was lynched? Or had he used it to get them to do what he wanted?

"I talked to your mom," I said. "I told her I'd help you come in without getting hurt."

I could feel his body react to what I was saying. He relaxed slightly and paused a moment.

"She's worried about you," I said. "Your sister too, but

she's got a funny way of showing it."

"Tracy's a stuck up bitch," he said.

I nodded my agreement.

"Let me help you. You were so close to getting out. Why'd you run?"

"You don't seem to understand your situation," he said. "I'm gonna—"

"I'm trying to understand," I said. "I want to help."

I listened for the approaching motor that signaled Merrill's return but didn't hear it. The only sounds besides our breathing were the unseen animals and insects all around us.

"It's a little late for that now," he said. "You should've helped me when you had the chance."

"When was that?"

"You know goddamn well when. You couldn't even be bothered to see me. Now I'm gonna show you how it felt."

"I would've seen you any time you asked. Why didn't you send me a request?"

"I did," he said.

"I never got it," I said.

"Bullshit," he yelled.

"You think I got it and just ignored it?" I asked.

"I think you're just trying to stay alive," he said. "You'd say anything."

"Have I ever ignored your requests before?"

Though housed at the work camp, his inmate requests regarding religion were sent to me.

He didn't say anything.

"You know me," I said. "You think I would—"

He wrapped his grimy hand around my mouth as he heard Merrill heading back toward us.

"Tell Mama I'm sorry," he said, "and don't come back out here again. Next time I'll kill you."

He then grabbed a handful of my hair, slammed my face

into the ground, jumped off me, and ran away.

I rolled over, wiping the dirt from my eyes, and tried to see which way he'd gone, but there was no sign of him anywhere.

I jumped to my feet and continued to look for him but got the same result.

When Merrill ran up I told him what had happened and we began making our way deeper into the swamp, looking for any indication of the direction he had gone.

We walked for well over a mile before we found anything, the swamp growing more dense, seemingly more impenetrable with every step.

Inside a channel that would have been filled with water if the river had been higher, we found a boot print. We couldn't be sure if he had just made it, but with all the rain lately, it couldn't have been there long.

Ten-foot-high mounds of dirt and clay formed the banks of the channel, and its soggy bottom had the texture of a recently dried-up riverbed.

Eventually the wind picked up and it began to rain. The breeze blowing down the channel caused the rain to slant in on us, pelting our hands and faces.

Deciding to return to the boat, we climbed out of the channel and headed back in what we thought was the direction of the river, though we couldn't be certain.

We had taken less than twenty steps on the other side of the channel wall when about a dozen men in camouflage fatigues jumped up from beneath ferns on the ground and out from behind trees, yelling and pointing M-16s at us.

Chapter Forty-one

Merrill and I both did what we were told, slowly raising our hands and standing still.

It was as if we had suddenly and surreally stepped into a war zone.

The soldiers, Navy SEALs from the look of them, were all dressed in full military field uniforms. In addition to camouflage fatigues, many of them wore camouflage headbands or floppy hats, but a few had helmets with shredded green and camouflage cloth meant to resemble grass and weeds. Ammunition belts crisscrossed their chests and their faces were painted black and green.

Of the twelve men, all were in their early to mid-twenties except for one. I assumed he was the commander. They looked weary and ragged but wild and wide-eyed, as if jolted back to full consciousness by a sudden adrenaline rush.

A few of the really young guys seemed jittery, their faces and hands twitching, and I realized how easily Merrill and I could be shot by accident.

"Steady men," the elder soldier said.

He wasn't much older, maybe late-twenties or early thirties, but he seemed far more mature.

"And if you're feeling tired and twitchy, why don't you take your fingers off the triggers," I suggested.

No one responded. Nor moved a finger.

"State your name and purpose for being out here," the elder one said.

We told him who we were, being sure to slip in the fact that my dad was the sheriff.

"You got ID?" he asked.

We nodded.

"Let's see it," he said. "Very slowly."

We handed our wallets to the guy standing closest to us and he passed them along to the guy standing next to the commander. He looked through our wallets and read the information on our driver's licenses out loud.

"There's also some business cards from Potter Correctional Institution that say 'John Jordan, Senior Chaplain' on them," he said.

"Okay, men," the commander said, "stand down."

They did.

"Sorry about that," the commander said, "but we're not used to seeing civilians this far back in the swamp and we're a little . . ."

"You Navy SEALs?" I asked.

He nodded. "We train out here because of how close the terrain is to certain countries where we carry out missions."

"I read something about that in the paper a while back," I said.

He frowned. "We're still not sure how that happened. Don't like to advertise the fact that we're here."

As we talked the rest of the men spread out around us, some standing, others sitting on the ground. By their position and posture I could tell some were standing guard.

The canopy of oak trees kept most of the rain off us but we were still getting wet.

No one seemed to notice.

"You have a camp somewhere out here?" I asked.

He patted the large backpack on the ground beside him.

"Carry it with us."

I nodded.

The approaching darkness brought with it a light, wispy fog that rolled in and hovered just above the ground around us.

"What the hell're you boys doin' this deep in the swamp?" one of the more Southern-sounding soldiers asked. "Y'all lost?"

"We were chasing an inmate who escaped," I said.

Their eyes grew wide and they exchanged glances. Those not on watch moved in closer.

"Tell us more about this inmate," the commander said.

"You seen him?" I asked.

He shook his head.

"He's a white guy a little shorter than me. Thicker. More muscular. Got a bad inmate haircut—"

"Looks sorta like yours," Merrill said with a smile.

He didn't return the smile. No one did. There was a new tension in the air now, its presence as palpable as the fog.

"He had on an inmate uniform at first, but now he's wearing street clothes," I said.

"How dangerous is he?" he asked.

I shrugged. "Not sure exactly. But he needs to be treated with extreme caution."

He shook his head, anger flaring in his eyes, as the muscles in his jaw tightened. "We'll catch the son of a bitch. Don't you worry about that."

"I wasn't asking you to catch him," I said. "We have rotating teams from the prison and local law enforcement searching the area."

"Nobody knows this place like we do," he said.

"If you happen to see him, let us know, but there's no need—"

"Oh, we're gonna catch the little cocksucker," he said, "and God help him when we do."

"We want to catch him without anyone getting hurt," I

said. "Including him."

"I can guarantee no more of my men will get hurt," he said.

One of the men nearby said, "Same can't be said for the convict."

I looked back at the commander. "No more of your men?"

"We're missing a man," he said. "And now we know why."

Chapter Forty-two

"You think the guy who was lynched is their missing man?" Dad asked.

It was later that night.

Showered and changed, Merrill and I had come to Rudy's to eat, which we were busy doing when Dad had arrived to talk to us about what we had learned on the river.

"Said he was black," Merrill said.

"If it's not him we've got another victim somewhere out there," I said.

Dad shook his head and frowned, his eyes narrowing with concern. I knew he never wanted anyone to die, that he took it personally if someone in his county on his watch did, but I also knew that at the moment he was also considering its impact on his chances at reelection.

"He's coming in tomorrow to see if he can identify him," I said, "but I doubt it's him."

"Why's that?" Dad asked.

"If our guy had been a SEAL we would've gotten a match on his prints."

Dad's frown deepened as he nodded absently.

"Unless they really not SEALs," Merrill said.

Dad's eyebrows shot up, his eyes widening.

I nodded. "They could be one of those units that don't exist."

"Shadow ops shit?" Merrill said. "Black holes. Secret prisons. Sub-contracted killers."

I nodded.

"For the sake of the homeland," he said. "We be takin' the terror to them."

Merrill and I sat on opposite sides of the booth, Dad in a chair at the end. The table between us was filled with varying sized plates, all with partially consumed food. We had a full-size plate for waffles and smaller plates for bacon, toast, and hash browns. Merrill was having coffee—and a lot of it. Carla had left the pot so he could refill as often as he liked—which was often. I was drinking Dr. Pepper.

"Of course they might not be government at all," I said. "They could just as easily be a paramilitary militia of some sort."

"Oh God, I hope to hell not," Dad said.

"Hell, they could be the ones doin' all the killin'," Merrill said. "Maybe Turtle saw something he wasn't supposed to. Maybe the other victim wasn't willing to go along with something they did."

"If you didn't find them convincing," Dad said, "why didn't you—"

"We found their machine guns very convincing," Merrill said.

Dad smiled.

Carla was at the counter doing her homework. We were the only people in the place—except for Rudy who was passed out in the back.

"Well we'll know more tomorrow," I said.

"If he doesn't show," Dad said, "what are the chances we'll be able to find them again?"

"Merrill and I walked straight to them today."

"You think Jensen was trying to lead you to them?" Dad asked. "Or them to you?"

I thought about it. It was an interesting proposition. "I guess he could've been," I said. "It hadn't crossed my mind."

"Think he wanted us to know they's there," Merrill said, "or wanted them to shoot us?"

It had stopped raining but the highway out front was still wet, the damp asphalt gleaming dully in passing headlights.

"Least we know he's still out there," Dad said. "We can intensify the search now. You think he's our killer?"

I shrugged. "Can't rule out the possibility. He's got a lot of rage."

"And yet he didn't kill you."

"That's 'cause he heard me coming," Merrill said with a smile.

And I realized how scarce his smile had been recently.

We were all quiet a moment.

A gust of wind outside scattered some wet leaves and trash around and made the plate glass window beside us creak with the strain.

"Merrill," Dad said, "did John talk to you about the primary?"

A sharp pang of guilt shot through me and some old familiar feelings of family betrayal rushed to the surface from the suppressed depths where they had been submerged.

"I haven't had a chance yet," I said. "I was going to tonight."

"I need your help," Dad said to Merrill. "I'm gonna get beat otherwise."

Merrill didn't say anything.

"I know one of the candidates is your cousin," he said, "but . . ."

"Not sure what I can do," Merrill said. "Let me think about it."

"I'm running out of time," he said. "The primary is Tuesday. Please. John and I really need you."

I felt uncomfortable and tried to think of a way to

change the subject.

"Did John tell you I found out the name of that minister from Marianna, the one you saw, and that he's still missing?"

Merrill nodded.

"We're gonna find out what happened," he said. "I promise you that. Once the election is over, we can really—if I'm still sheriff—we can really concentrate on the case."

Dad was a good, decent, man, and I hated to see him like this. I knew he was just trying to get reelected, that it was a means to an end, but I sat there wishing there could be other means or that he could be less concerned about the end.

We were quiet again, the tension in the air between us apparent.

Finally, Dad stood and said, "Well, I've got to go. Please think about what I said. Things could be better in our county, and I'm working on it, but they could be a whole hell of lot worse too. A hell of a lot worse."

He took a few steps away, then came back. "I know this is going to sound crazy and paranoid, but I can't help but wonder if what's happening—the timing and the manner and all—has something to do with the election."

I thought about it. I was only mildly surprised by Dad's paranoia. There was a certain egocentric woundedness in him that surfaced from time to time in the form of a kind of victimhood. What he'd just said was a slightly elevated form of that.

What he was saying was farfetched and improbable, but not entirely impossible, not unthinkable. Far stranger things had been done for far lower stakes.

"Anything's possible," I said.

"Well, goodnight," he said.

He patted Carla on the back as he walked past her and dropped money on the counter beside her for our food. He hadn't eaten.

"Sorry about that," I said.

Merrill shook his head and waved off my apology.

"I feel so sorry for him," I said.

He nodded. "I understand," he said. "He a good man as far as it go."

I nodded.

"But he also racist," he said.

I frowned and nodded. "Not nearly as much as many of his generation around here," I said, "but yeah, he is."

"If you ask me to campaign for him," he said, "I will."

I thought about all my dad had done for me over the years and I was flooded with feelings of gratitude, sadness, and guilt.

I shook my head. "I won't," I said. "I can't. But he's right. Things could be a hell of a lot worse and I think objectively—at least as objectively as I can be—he's the best candidate."

Merrill nodded. "I'll see what I can do. And John, thanks for not asking."

"There is something I do want to ask you," I said.

"Shoot."

"Are you okay?"

He didn't say anything.

"I feel like I haven't been a very good friend lately," I said. "I've been worried about you. I can tell something's wrong. Just wondered what and what I could do."

He nodded. "Nothing you can do right now."

"You sure?" I asked. "I can do a lot of shit."

He smiled and it was nice to see. "I'm sure."

"You'll let me know if that changes?"

"I will," he said. "And John, thanks for asking."

Chapter Forty-three

As soon as Merrill left, Carla came over to the booth and slid in across from me.

"How's your mom?" she asked.

I told her, aware I was talking to a young girl who had no idea where her mother was. As I did I was reminded again of just how much parents injure their children. Carla was smart, strong, and beautiful, but she was also insecure, fearful of abandonment, and uncomfortable with true intimacy—and probably would be for the rest of her life. There are some truly scary things in the world but nothing can compare to the damage done by parents in the formative years of their children's lives. This, more than any other factor, was the reason Anna's pregnancy meant there was no hope of us ever being together. At least not in this life.

"You think she'll get a transplant in time?"

I shrugged. "It's not looking good."

She nodded and frowned, then looked down. When she looked up there were tears in her eyes and she said, "I'm sorry."

"Thanks," I said.

I knew she was crying about far more than my mom, and I was glad to see her tears. They were rare—and she was someone with more than her fair share of things to cry about.

The lights of the diner were dim—something Rudy had

devised to save a little more money, and as usual, it was cold.
If Rudy really wanted to save money all he'd have to do was
bump up the thermostat, but, in addition to being overweight
and always overheated, he was convinced, or wanted to be, that
it generated more coffee sales and kept his daughter awake at
night.

Carla and I were alone. The jukebox sat silently by.
Except for the occasional vehicle passing on the highway
outside, it was as if we were the only two people left in the wide
world.

Carla lingered, periodically wiping her eyes and sniffling,
and I knew she had something she needed to talk about.

I waited.

She would get to it when she was ready. She always did.

Eventually, she said, "Know how we have stories that
circulate around here? Sort of like rural legends?"

I nodded.

She turned and looked over her shoulder out into the
darkness, and I couldn't tell if she was scared or expecting
someone.

"There's a new one a lot of the kids are talking about,"
she said. "No one has said it happened to them, but so many
are talking about it and they all say the same thing."

"What are they saying?"

"That a guy is abducting people—teenage boys, I
think—drugging them or knocking them out and taking them
to a . . . they call it the dungeon. It's like a torture chamber."

She shivered and started to cry again and I thought I
knew where this was going.

"After a few days, he drops them off in a secluded place,
and they do their best to pretend like it never happened."

I was skeptical. It sounded more like rural legend
than anything else, and I couldn't imagine something like this
wouldn't get out. I would check with Dad to see of any parents
had reported their kids missing, only to get them back later.

"Why haven't the parents or the school reported it?" I asked.

She shrugged. "The guys it's happened to are pretty much on their own. And he never keeps them for long. They just act like they spent a few nights with a friend."

Very slowly and gently, I said, "Do you think this happened to Cody?"

I recalled her saying her boyfriend, Cody Gaskin, had disappeared for three days and not been the same since he got back.

She started crying harder and nodded.

"He's so different, so angry. He won't talk to me about where he went or what he did. He just says it's none of my business and if I ask him again he's going to . . . do things to me."

My empathy for Cody and his experience quickly vanished, my compassion turning to anger, and I was filled with the desire to do a few things to him.

She turned and looked outside again. "He's supposed to be coming over tonight. Will you talk to him?"

I nodded. "No matter how much you love him," I said, "or what he may have been through, you can't let him talk to you that way. You can't be in a relationship with someone who would abuse you in any way—even verbal threats."

"I know," she said. "I'm just scared if I break up with him . . ."

"I understand," I said. "I'll encourage him not to do anything stupid."

She tried to smile, but only partly pulled it off.

"What time is he coming?" I asked.

"He should have already been here," she said. "He's probably waiting for you to leave."

"You want me to park my pimp ride around back?" I asked.

She looked out into the darkness again. "He could be

watching us right now," she said. "Why don't you drive away—just don't go far—then come back when he shows up."

I did.

When I walked back into Rudy's ten minutes later, Cody rolled his eyes, stood up from the booth he was sitting in with Carla, and said, "I'm outta here."

"Sit down, Cody," I said.

He didn't move.

"Carla, would you mind fixing us some coffee?"

She stood, and eased past Cody as if she expected him to hit her.

I walked over toward him.

"Sit down," I said, my voice firm but not menacing. Not yet.

Cody Gaskin was high school football quarterback tough. Beneath his red-and-white letterman jacket was the result of many hours spent in the weight room and taking questionable supplements. He had lived an entitled, indulged life and wasn't used to being told what to do—especially by a trailer trash convict preacher.

If he'd been abducted and held, his absence would have gone unremarked because he was allowed to do whatever he wanted, coming and going as he liked.

If Carla was right about what had happened to him, then for the first time since infancy, Cody had known what it was like to be powerless. I tried to remind myself of what he had possibly been through to balance the anger I felt toward him.

"I just want to talk to you."

He turned and glared at Carla but she wasn't looking at him.

"Cody," I said, "if you want to glare at someone, glare at me."

I stepped closer, he dropped into the booth, and I slid in across from him.

Carla brought our coffee, careful not to stand too close

to Cody as she placed the cups and saucers on the table. This time he didn't look at her.

"Carla, why don't you join us?" I said.

Her eyes widened and she hesitated.

"Cody's not going to do anything to you," I said. "You don't have anything to worry about. Right Cody?"

Cody didn't say anything.

I stood and Carla slid in on my side of the booth. I sat down beside her.

Cody was looking down at the table, his face tight and red, his lips pursed.

"What happened to you, Cody?" I asked.

He didn't say anything.

"Were you taken? Held for a while? Assaulted?"

He still didn't say anything but the tremors in his hands and the moistness in his eyes told me what I needed to know.

"I'm sure what happened to you had to be beyond horrible," I said, "and I'm very sorry. We're going to catch the guy who did it to you and make sure he doesn't do anything like that to anyone ever again. But Cody, if you ever threaten Carla again, I'll put you in the hospital. And things will only escalate from there."

He didn't say anything and didn't look up.

"Carla, do you wish to continue dating Cody?" I asked.

She hesitated a long moment then shook her head. "Not right now," she said. "Maybe later when . . . after . . ."

"Do you understand?" I asked Cody.

After a moment, he nodded his head, but still didn't look up.

"Okay," I said, standing, "Carla, why don't you go get some rest. Cody and I have a few things to discuss."

She stood and looked down at him. "I'm sorry," she whispered. "I love you."

Cody's family was solidly middle class, which in an economically depressed area like ours, where the highest earners are teachers and correctional officers, made him a "rich" kid. He was also attractive, popular, and the star quarterback. Carla was poor, not involved in any extracurricular activities because she had to work so much, and though not unpopular, she wasn't a cheerleader, wasn't allowed completely inside the cool kids clique.

As I sat back down and waited for Carla to make her way into the back, I wondered how much this social and economic dynamic was involved in what Carla was calling love.

"Look at me like a man," I said.

He looked up, anger burning in his narrowed eyes.

"We're going to get you some help," I said. "And we're going to catch the man who did this to you. But the first step is being honest about what happened. My first priority in this situation is Carla, but you are my second. I won't judge you. I won't think any less of you. I've spent my life working with people who've gone through similar things. What happened to you is not your fault. It's about evil, about a sick individual who has given himself over to it. None of that has anything to do with you. So, tell me what happened?"

He didn't say anything.

I sipped some coffee and waited.

I wound up waiting a long time, but eventually something inside him broke loose, and he began to cry. I wasn't able to make out all of his tearful story, but I got a lot— including the most telling line of all: "The worst thing of all was that he made me do the stuff to myself."

Chapter Forty-four

"That means the rapist isn't an inmate, right?" Anna asked.

We were in the Monte Carlo heading toward Panama City Beach to talk to the owner of Air Ads Inc.

It was midday, the sun directly overhead shrouded in rain clouds, thunder rumbling in the distance.

The warden had reluctantly approved my request to use a couple of hours of my comp time—and only because I was visiting my mom, which I would be after going to Air Ads Inc.

Before approving the request, he had given me a lecture about the importance of being at the institution and, as a department head, setting a good example. I agreed with him and reminded him that the reason I had so much comp time was because of how much of my recent life had been spent at the prison, and that I only had one mother so this shouldn't be an issue in the future. I felt guilty for using Mom as an excuse and not being completely honest, until he told me to make sure that it wasn't.

"Probably," I said, "but not positively."

As usual 23rd Street was crowded, the multiple stoplights adding to the congestion of the slow-moving traffic. The parking lots of the ubiquitous chain restaurants were packed, cars of hungry workers circling in search of an empty slot, the precious minutes of their lunch hours ticking away.

"How could it be an inmate?"

"It would be difficult," I said, "but Cody said the guy only came to the place he holds them periodically. It's not inconceivable that an inmate assigned to a negligent city worker on an outside work crew could be doing it. Some of them don't really supervise at all—especially if the inmate's been working for them a long time. When the inmate is alone, he could use the city truck to snatch the kid and take him to an abandoned building or empty river camp, then come back each day for another session, and eventually let him go. Not the most probable scenario. Just saying it's not impossible."

"We've certainly had negligent supervisors before," she said, "but . . ."

"It's about as likely as someone committing the murders to make Dad look bad and lose the election," I said. "It's possible, but . . ."

"Does he think that?"

I shrugged. "It's crossed his mind. We can't rule either of them out completely but we need to focus on other possibilities. Lisa's creating a new list of rape suspects from staff, correctional officers, and inmates on an outside work crew."

"That should narrow it down greatly," she said.

Classes were back in and the parking lots of Gulf Coast State College's main campus were full. As we rose atop Hathaway Bridge amid a steady flow of traffic in both directions, I slowed and looked out over the bay. The waters were choppy, a seemingly infinite number of whitecaps bouncing, rocking, jostling. The overcast day drained much of the vivid color from what was normally a picturesque announcement that crossing the bridge from Panama City to Panama City Beach signaled a transition between a small panhandle town and a world famous vacation destination, between the monotony of responsibility and the variety of possibility.

"How're you feeling?" I asked.

She frowned and shrugged.

"Any morning sickness?"

"A little. And a little afternoon. A little evening. I'm usually so nauseous at night that the only relief I can get is to go to sleep. Eating helps but only briefly. No wonder us preggos get so fat."

"You won't be fat," I said. "You'll be pregnant, and there's nothing in this world more beautiful than a pregnant woman."

She smiled. "Thank you. You're sweet."

"I'm serious," I said.

The traffic on Back Beach moved a lot quicker than in town and soon we were passing the driving range and the defunct independent Charismatic church whose preacher's extravagant lifestyle and acrimonious divorce had bankrupted far more than its budget.

"I'm worried," she said.

"About?"

"I'm afraid all my anxiety and negative feelings about this pregnancy will affect the baby," she said.

I nodded.

"Tell me they won't," she said.

I smiled. "You'll work through them before they have a chance to," I said.

"Are you mad at me?"

I shook my head.

"You don't hate me?"

"Of course not. I love you."

We were silent a moment, and feeling the need to move away a bit from what I'd just said, I added, "You're gonna make a wonderful mother."

She looked at me for a long moment, her smile wide and warm, her deep brown eyes intelligent and intense, her smooth skin and countenance radiant, and time did what it does when I'm with her and the next thing I knew we had reached Air Ads Inc.

Chapter Forty-five

Air Ads Inc. consisted of a grass runway, two planes, and a small portable office trailer. It was situated off the highway behind a few rows of pine trees that served as a buffer between it and the traffic on Highway 98.

A dirt road with several deep ruts and potholes led from the highway through the trees to the small operation.

When we pulled up in the Monte Carlo an older man with a sun-damaged face and a long gray ponytail stopped working on one of the planes to stare at us suspiciously.

"I think my car is being subjected to racial profiling," I said.

Anna laughed.

"Junior," he yelled, as I opened my door.

"John," I yelled back, as I got out of the car.

"My bad," he said. "Thought you were someone else."

"I am," I said. "Tom around?"

"Inside," he yelled, and went back to work.

"I think he's disappointed," Anna said.

"I get that a lot," I said.

We found a heavy blond teenage girl inside with one of the most accomplished attitudes of indifference I'd ever seen. She didn't even speak to us when we walked into the small room. To the extent she acknowledged our presence, she seemed angry at the intrusion, though she wasn't even pretending to work. She was texting on a small cell phone with her thumbs.

We waited for a few minutes, as if not wanting to interrupt her work, but she never stopped or looked up once since we had first walked through the door.

"Tom in?" I asked.

She looked up and glared at me, her pale blue eyes narrowing angrily, then she jerked her head toward a door behind her in the right corner.

"Thanks," I said.

We walked in Tom's office to find him on the phone. Cupping his hand over the receiver, he said, "Give me one minute. I'll be right with you."

He uncupped the receiver then recupped it again. "Have a seat—if you can make a space for yourself."

His small office consisted of a cheap desk, a credenza, and a single small bookshelf, and was cluttered and overcrowded. Piles and stacks of aerial maps, contracts, weather reports, and three-ring binders littered every available surface and several places on the floor. An aquarium with everything but water and fish sat in one corner, several rolled-up banners in the other.

We cleared piles of paper from the chairs across from his desk and sat down.

"Whatever you're paying the girl out front," I said when he got off the phone, "it's too much."

He smiled. "She's a charmer, isn't she?"

"A couple of other words came to mind," Anna said.

Since we had entered his office, Tom Brown had found it difficult not to look at Anna. He tried to steal glances at her, to feast his eyes surreptitiously, but it only drew more attention to his schoolboy reaction to her beauty.

"Well if it's any consolation," he said, "she's not getting a dime from me. She's a, ah, friend of my son's who's getting community service credit for sitting in there talking on her cell phone and doing her nails all day. Our justice system in action."

"Inaction is right," Anna said.

He smiled but it was obvious he didn't get it.

"So what can I do for you two? Need some inexpensive, cost-effective advertising on the beach?"

"I read about your plane that went down last week," I said.

He instantly became wary, defensive.

"Uh huh," he said.

"I thought I saw a similar one in trouble a week and a half or so ago," I said, "and I wondered if it was one of yours?"

"Where was this?" he asked.

I gave him all the details and what I thought I saw.

"And you're sure it didn't have a banner?" he asked.

I nodded. "When I read that the first thing your pilots do when they get into trouble is drop their banner, I thought that maybe the plane I saw was one of yours."

He shook his head. "That's too far east to have been one of mine," he said.

"And you're not missing any planes?"

He shook his head.

"Are there any other companies like yours in the area?" I asked. "Maybe more to the east."

He shook his head. "I'm the only one. And the only business is on the beach."

"Okay," I said. "Thanks for your time."

Anna and I stood to leave. He stood and extended his hand. First to Anna, then to me.

"If you don't mind me asking, why does it matter whose plane it was?" he said.

I shrugged. "I'd just like to know. I thought it may have gone down. It probably has nothing to do with the escape or the murders, but we won't know for sure until we find out whose it was and why they were there."

"It's just a little quirk of his," Anna said. "Cute, isn't it?"

"Well good luck," he said.

When we walked back out into the office, we found the overweight blond teenager doing even less than when we had arrived.

"No message to respond to?" I asked.

"Battery's dead," she said. "Charger's in the car."

"Where's your car?" Anna asked.

"Out there," she said, jerking her head toward the front door.

"All the way out there?" I asked.

She didn't say anything, as if to do so required too much energy.

I laid my card on her desk. "In case he thinks of anything else," I said.

"Or you think of anything at all," Anna said.

Chapter Forty-six

Fisher and Son was the only funeral home in Potter County. Located in an old two-story clapboard house with a wide wraparound veranda, it was situated on the back of a large lot beneath enormous Spanish moss-draped oak trees. As kids growing up in Pottersville, we always suspected it was haunted, and often dared each other to sneak into it—especially on Halloween.

Nathan Fisher lived upstairs and operated the business beneath. He lived alone since his son died and his wife left him, and was a source of small-town talk—how could a normal person live with all those bodies? What exactly was his relationship with them? He had never been accused of anything or even received a single complaint over the years, but that didn't prevent people from some highly imaginative speculation.

Since Potter County wasn't large enough to have a morgue, bodies were housed by Fisher, and occasionally autopsies were performed in his prep room. This didn't happen often, but the county contract helped Fisher survive as more and more people used the services of large homes in Tallahassee and Panama City.

When I arrived at Fisher's I found Nathan in the parlor playing a video game on a small handheld device. As he stood, he quickly slipped the player into the inside coat pocket of his ill-fitting, inexpensive, carbon-dated black suit.

"Sorry about that. You're a little early."

Nathan Fisher was a tall, gaunt, nervous man with pale skin and dark features. His long fingers were narrow, his hands cold and clammy, his handshake limp. As usual, his breath smelled of equal parts cigarettes and mouthwash.

I had dropped Anna off after leaving Air Ads Inc. and had come straight here. Fearing I was running late, I had driven far faster than I normally did—actually the borrowed car enabled me to drive far faster than my truck had been capable of doing.

"The others are on the way," I said.

He nodded. "Would you like anything?" he asked. "Coffee or something?"

"No thank you," I said.

"How're things at the prison?" he asked.

I never quite knew what to say to that. "About the same I guess."

"A lot of people don't understand why you do it," he said. "The whole chaplain thing. But I do."

I smiled politely and nodded.

"Whatever's left after we die is not us," he said. "It's not. And if we're spirits, then we had to be created by a spirit, and that means there's got to be a God."

Before he could say anything else, Dad and the others arrived.

Dad looked weary and stressed, the tension visible in the lines of his narrow-eyed scowl and the deep crevice just above the bridge of his nose. I could tell by the way he walked he wanted to get this over with as quickly as possible.

The man with him, Chuck, the SEAL commander I had met the day before, looked very different cleaned up and in his civilian clothes.

Once everyone had been introduced and Nathan made his final preparations, we all stepped into the viewing room for Chuck to see if he could identify the lynching victim.

When Nathan pulled back the sheet to reveal the face of the man who had been beaten to death and then hanged, Chuck shook his head.

"That's not him," he said.

"You're sure?" Dad asked.

He narrowed his eyes and gave Dad a look of incredulity. "Positive."

"Okay," Dad said. "I guess we're done here. Thank you, Nathan."

As we walked back through the parlor toward our vehicles, Chuck said, "I don't know whether to be relieved or more worried."

"You do what you like," Dad said, "but I'm gonna go with more worried."

As we stepped out onto the veranda Chuck's phone rang, and he stopped to answer it. I could tell by his reaction that it was bad news. When he finished the call, he slowly closed his phone and slipped it back into his pocket.

"They've found him," he said.

Chapter Forty-seven

In what must have appeared to observers to be a strange alternate reality, it looked like I, in my pimped-out ride, was chasing Dad, in his siren-screeching, emergency light-flashing sheriff's truck, but no one pulled me over and we made good time.

As we neared the landing my phone rang. It was Carla.

"How fast can you get to the landing?" she asked.

"Very," I said. "Why?"

"Cody's real upset," she said. "He needs to talk to you."

"I'll be right there," I said. "Are you with him?"

She hesitated and I knew she was.

"I thought it was over and you were going to stay away from him?"

"I know," she said, sighing heavily. "But you know how these things are."

"Yes, I do," I said. "Which is why I wanted you to stay away from him."

"Just get here as fast as you can," she said.

Before she had finished saying it I was pulling into the landing, and could see her sitting next to Cody under one of the pavilions near the playground.

The landing was empty except for a few trucks and boat trailers scattered throughout. Besides Carla and Cody, the only other people visible were an elderly couple on the dock.

It had rained earlier and the pavement and ground still held puddles, the overcast day impotent to dry them up.

When I reached them, Cody looked at Carla, who looked up at me and said, "I'll let you two talk. If you need me, I'll be over there." She nodded toward the swings.

I sat down beside Cody and waited. In a few moments I realized that the seat was wet and now so were my pants.

Dad and Chuck were standing over near the boat launch, waiting, as Jake backed the search and rescue boat toward the ramp.

"You okay?" I asked.

He nodded, though it was obvious he was not.

His skin was colorless and clammy, his left eye twitching.

"What happened?"

"Carla and me came here after school," he said. "Just to talk. I just needed to see her. I wasn't tryin' to get back with her or nothin', and I swear I wouldn't hurt her for anything."

I nodded, glancing over at Carla sitting in one of the swings, her feet dragging along in the dirt as she slowly moved back and forth.

"As we sat here talking, with our backs to the river, I heard something that brought it all back—it was as if I was there again, chained up in the dark about to be made to do things to myself."

"What did you hear?"

"A boat passing by on the river," he said. "That's all. I guess I had forgotten. Hell, I've been tryin' to block the whole thing out."

"So wherever you were it was close to the river," I said.

He nodded.

With the search and rescue boat in the water, Jake pulled the truck and boat trailer up off the ramp and parked in a nearby space. He rejoined the others and I could tell they were waiting for me, could feel their impatience.

"Can you remember anything else about it?" I asked.

"It was damp and smelled bad. Water was dripping somewhere nearby, and I got the feeling that it was down underground or something."

"Do you remember how you got away?" I asked.

He shook his head. "I just remember waking up at the dump."

"Okay," I said. "This really helps. We're going to catch him. You're helping us keep him from doing this to anybody else. Are you still talking to the counselor?"

He nodded.

"Is it helping?"

He shrugged.

"It will," I said. "Keep it up."

"Yes sir."

"Can you think of anything else?" I asked. "I know it's painful and you don't want to, but it helps. It really does—and not just me."

He shook his head then hesitated. "Why does he . . . make you do that stuff?" he asked. "Is it because he can't . . . ."

"He didn't . . . do anything to you?" I asked.

He shook his head. "Just made me do sick shit to myself."

"Well he never will again," I said. "You don't have to worry about that. We're going to catch him soon."

"JOHN," Dad yelled from the ramp. "WE'VE GOT TO GO."

I nodded and waved but didn't stand up.

"Do I have to stay away from Carla?" he asked.

"That's up to Carla," I said, then looked over at her. "But she doesn't seem to want you to."

He exhaled, his face registering relief, his body relaxing a bit, and his lips twitched briefly with the faintest hint of a smile.

Chapter Forty-eight

The gray day made the river look darker and dirty, its banks dull.

The breeze had picked up and the boat bounced and bumped along the wide, windswept waters. Though we were driving against the wind, Jake drove as fast as the small boat would go, and it stung our faces and watered our eyes.

Thankfully, we didn't have to go far.

The area where all the attention was focused was in the river in front of the large sand dune created by the dredging the Corps of Engineers did. It was over seventy-five feet high and three hundred feet wide—a cascading mountain of golden riverbed sand that would soon wash back into the water.

Three boats formed a triangle around what I gathered was the watery crime scene—Robert Pridgeon's game warden boat on the side closest to us, Todd and Shane in the other search and rescue boat, and half a dozen of the SEALs in a boat opposite them.

We pulled up next to Robert.

"Whatta we got?" Dad asked.

"Submerged boat," Robert said, nodding toward a place in the river between their three boats. One corner of one side stuck out just above the surface at the spot he had indicated. "There's a body in it."

"Is it my missing man?" Chuck asked.

"According to them," he said, jerking his head toward the SEAL team.

"FDLE is on the way," Dad said.

"You wanna wait for them or go ahead and get it up?"

"How the hell we gonna do that?" Jake asked.

"Do it all the time," Robert said. "Take out the plug, hook a line to the bow and pull it with my boat. It will slowly rise up, water draining out the sides and through the hole. Once it's up pop the plug back in."

"Is the body secure enough for us to do that?" Dad asked.

"I think so," he said.

"Can you see it from the surface?"

He nodded.

"Okay," Dad said, "let's take a look, then we'll pull it up."

Jake switched from the powerful outboard motor to the small trolling motor, and slowly eased us up next to the submerged vessel. It was a small aluminum boat with built-in bench seats and no motor.

Visibility was low but we could see through the surface of the windy water to the horror below.

A naked black man in his late twenties was lying in the boat on his back in a spread eagle position, his wrists and ankles strapped to the seats with nylon rope.

As we looked at him no one said anything, but I could tell by Chuck's reaction he knew the man.

"That him?" Dad asked.

He nodded.

"What's his name?" I asked.

"Scott," he said, his voice tight and hoarse. "Scott Colvin. He was a good man."

I nodded.

"Okay," Dad said. "Let's get him up."

Jake started the trolling motor and swung us back around

beside Robert's game warden boat.

"IS IT HIM?" one of the SEALs yelled from their boat.

Chuck nodded.

Looking over at the SEALs I noticed how different their boat was from the one Colvin was in.

"Whose boat is that?" I asked.

Chuck shrugged. "Don't know."

Robert and Dad both looked at him, eyebrows raised.

"You don't know who it belongs to?" Dad asked.

"No idea," Chuck said.

"Think it belongs to the killer?" Jake asked.

"You mean the dead man walking?" Chuck said.

"We'll know soon enough," Robert said.

"How?" Jake asked.

"Let's get it up and I'll show you."

After helping Robert secure his towing chain to the submerged boat and removing its plug, we pulled over close to the other two boats and watched as he slowly brought up the submerged craft. The process looked like a novice water skier trying shakily to break the surface of the water and remain on his feet—Robert gunning his engine to get the small aluminum boat up, the water resisting, as if the river was reluctant to release it for some reason.

Once he got it to the surface, we raced over behind it and put the plug back in. There was still some water in the boat but not enough to sink it or hinder the investigation.

"Why don't we pull it on in to the landing and examine it there?" Robert asked. "Be a hell of a lot easier than trying to do it out here on the water."

"We'll have to deal with gawkers," Dad said, "but the convenience'll make it worth it."

"We can handle 'em," Jake said.

Before we left, Chuck ordered his men back to base and told them he'd return as soon as he could.

Robert towed the aluminum boat with the body still

inside it carefully and slowly to the landing.

We followed closely behind. As we did, I found myself praying that Cody and Carla would be gone by the time we got there. This was the last thing Cody needed to see right now.

Thankfully, when we arrived at the landing it was empty.

Securing our boats to the dock, we used Jake's truck and trailer to pull the other boat ashore so we could begin to examine it. Jake drove over to the back side of the parking lot and Robert and Dad parked their vehicles a few feet in front of the boat with their emergency lights flashing.

The body had been in the water a while, and would have floated to the surface if it hadn't been tied down. It was bloated and disfigured and had a grayish, almost colorless tint to it. There were no obvious signs of trauma on the body and nothing on it or in the boat that could tell us how he died or who might have done it.

We turned our attention back to the boat as Robert began to examine it.

Walking along the exterior, looking closely at it, he said, "There are over a million boats registered in Florida this year. And every one has a registration sticker with a FL number on it."

We all searched the exterior of the boat for the registration sticker. It didn't have one.

"There's something sticky right here," Jake said, pointing to a small square of rosin-like residue.

Robert walked over, looked at it, and nodded. "That's where it was."

"Now what?" Jake asked.

"Every boat manufactured has a HIN."

"A what?" Jake asked.

"A hull identification number. Like a car's VIN. It'll tell us who bought the boat. Homemade boats don't have them— and we have a lot of those around here—but it's obvious this isn't one of them."

"Was this it?" Shane asked.

We joined him at the back of the boat and looked at scratch marks in the aluminum hull.

"Somebody's filed it off," Todd said.

"So now what?" Jake asked.

"Now," Robert said, "we call the manufacturer and ask them where the other HIN is."

"Whatta you mean?" Shane said.

"Every manufactured boat has a hidden HIN," Robert said. "All we have to do is find out where this manufacturer hides theirs."

Chapter Forty-nine

When I got home late that night, the first indication that something was wrong reminded me of the most famous of the Sherlock Holmes stories. I found it more than a little curious that my newly acquired hound didn't bark.

Normally he ran up to greet me regardless of the time, barking loudly and wetting himself.

Tonight I was greeted only by the normal nocturnal noises of rural North Florida.

I stood for a moment and listened, then began to call for him. "Walker," I said, then whistled. "Walker. Here Walker."

He didn't come, and when I walked around to the back of my trailer I knew why.

The faint light from the security lamp hanging from the top of my meter pole and the way the dark night soaked it up only added to the shock and horror of the scene.

Written in blood on the aluminum of the back wall of my trailer were the words Stay Off The River.

The blood had come from Walker, who was hanging by his blood-soaked neck from the limb of a nearby oak tree.

After carefully looking around to make sure whoever had left me the message was gone, I walked inside and called the sheriff's office, then walked back outside and waited for them to arrive.

I had enjoyed having Walker around and had felt good about the way he had been recovering, but as bad as I felt for how he had suffered and the way he had died, that was all I felt. I didn't feel any real sense of loss—and hadn't at the death of a pet since childhood. I'm not exactly sure of the reason, though I suspect it's an unconscious reflex at how short their lives can be—especially outside pets, which is all my family has ever had.

Merrill arrived ahead of Dad and the deputies. He had heard the response to my call on his scanner.

"Got damn, John," he said, "somebody done lynched your damn dog."

I smiled.

"Sorry," he said. "I know it all sad and shit, but damn, man."

"I know."

"How you respond to somethin' like this? Find the dude and fuck up his dog?"

Dad, Jake, Fred Goodwin, and a few other deputies arrived and began to process the scene.

As Dad looked at the writing on the trailer he said, "You think this is from our guy?"

I shrugged.

"Who else?" Jake asked.

"Just doesn't seem like his style," I said. "Killing me, yes, but killing my dog and leaving me a message . . ."

"Most serial killers stick within one species group," Merrill said with only the briefest flash of a smile.

"If it's him we must be getting close," Fred said.

"If that's true," I said, "why just threaten me? I don't think we're close, but if we are, I'm certainly no closer than any one of you."

"Good point," Dad said.

"You live the closest to the river," Merrill said. "And hell, maybe he was gonna write that it was to all of us and just ran out of blood."

Fred narrowed his eyes and nodded slowly. "Or time," he said as if Merrill had been serious.

Merrill looked at me and smiled.

"Could be Jensen," Dad said. "Or the SEALs. One of them could be the killer. Or all of 'em. Or it could be someone who has nothing to do with the case. You could have gotten close to someone's meth lab or marijuana crop. It could be anybody."

I nodded.

"So what you gonna do?" Merrill asked. "'Sides get another dog?"

"Stay off the river," I said.

"That's probably best," Fred said, as if I had been serious too. "For a while anyway. At least until we—"

"Fred," Dad said. "He's joking."

"Oh," he said. "Well, it's probably not a bad idea. I mean—"

"It's okay," Merrill said. "He got no other pets. Nothing else to lose."

My phone rang inside my pocket, its electronic alert sounding odd and out of place in the late quiet night.

"Maybe that's him," Fred said.

"Yeah," Merrill said. "Callin' with the rest of the message."

I walked away from the others and answered it.

"You the one looking for Junior?" she asked.

Where had I heard that voice before?

"What?"

"This the guy who talked to Tom about Junior?" she said.

Then I realized it was the community hours receptionist from Air Ads Inc., which made me remember that when I had first pulled up out there the guy working on the plane thought I was Junior.

"I came by and asked Tom about a plane going down," I said.

"Have you found him?"

"Who?" I asked.

"Junior," she said.

"Junior who?" I asked.

"Tom's son," she said. "Do you know where he's at?"

"No," I said. "I don't."

"Did his plane go down?" she asked. "He okay? He ain't in jail or nothin', is he? Your card says *prison* on it."

"I'm embarrassed to admit it," I said, "but you've lost me. Let's back up a minute. Junior is Tom Brown's son?"

"Well, his adopted son, yeah."

"And he's missing?"

"Uh huh."

"And so's his plane?"

"Well," she said, "it's Tom's plane, but yeah."

"How long's he been missing?" I asked.

"'Bout two weeks," she said.

"Why didn't Tom say anything when I asked him?" I said. "Has he reported Junior missing?"

"Junior stays in trouble. Always got some big plan to get rich and retire to the Keys. I'm real worried about him this time though. He usually shows back up by now. Have you seen him?"

I thought about it.

"I just might have," I said.

Chapter Fifty

The Cajun Café was a rarity in a town like Pottersville. Going far beyond the standard small Southern town fare of hamburgers, fried chicken, pork chops, and meatloaf, it served the best Cajun food this side of New Orleans. The chef could be successful anywhere. Thankfully she only wanted to live in Pottersville.

Amid other correctional officers and prison staff who had the same hour for lunch we did, Merrill and I were sitting with DeLisa Lopez at a table in the front near the large plate glass windows.

It was bright and hot.

Every time I looked through the window, I had to squint, and when I looked back into the restaurant it took a moment for my eyes to adjust.

Across Main Street the Potter State Bank sign said it was nearly ninety degrees. With the sun slanting in through the window and the number of patrons crowded into such a small area, the air conditioner was finding it difficult to keep up. Of course the spicy shrimp creole didn't help any.

"Here's the updated list," Lisa said. "The only inmates on it are the ones who work outside the gate."

She placed a copy of the list between us at an angle on the one small corner of the table without glasses, plates, or moisture on it.

We both turned our heads at an angle similar to that of the paper and looked down at it.

"These two are the inmates," she said, pointing to the two names off to the side by themselves. "Wayne Booth and James Frey."

I had been alone in the sanctuary of the chapel, lights off, contemplating the two cases in the quiet, when Lisa had called and suggested we look at the list over lunch. Time alone in the chapel was far more scarce since Chaplain Singer had started, and I was reluctant to give it up—not only because of how much I was enjoying it, but how the time to process things was helping the fragments begin to take form.

Suddenly I became aware that someone had said something to me that I hadn't responded to.

I looked from Lisa to Merrill.

"You okay?" she asked.

"Sorry. Just a little distracted."

"I heard about your dog," she said. "I'm so—"

"Ain't the dog," Merrill said. "That look mean he figuring shit out."

Lisa looked at me, her eyes wide beneath arched eyebrows.

I frowned and shook my head. "Just the very vague beginnings of some farfetched theories. Go ahead. I'm sorry."

"I'll get to that in a minute," she said. "Does it have to do with Anna too?"

"Everything has to do with her where he's concerned," Merrill said.

I nodded.

"Wanna talk about it some more?"

"I've let go," I said. "Let her go. Really and truly. Completely this time. And I'm still grieving. And that grief is always with me no matter what else I'm doing. Sort of like a low-grade fever. That's it. That's all it is."

"Sure you don't want to talk about it?"

I nodded. "Only the case right now."

She nodded. "When you're ready I'm here. Okay. So . . . the rest of the list is made up of staff and COs. The ones at the top are the ones we know the least about. The ones at the bottom are the least likely."

We looked at the list again. I was having a hard time focusing on it.

As I pushed my bowl of creole forward I noticed that Lisa had stopped nibbling on her red beans and rice, but Merrill's work on his shrimp po boy showed no signs of slowing.

Our waitress, a sweet but slow early twenties single mom working on her GED in night school, hadn't been by our table in a while and all that remained in the bottom of our glasses was a small amount of a watered-down brandy-looking substance formed from melting ice and a touch of sweet tea.

I glanced outside again.

Across the street a slow-moving elderly man everyone in town called Uncle Charlie shuffled down the walkway beneath the bank's sign toward the entrance. When he finally got there, he pulled on the left door to discover that he was either too weak to open it or it was locked.

When I looked back in I could see Sandy Hartman watching me from his table near the back. A few minutes later when Merrill went to the restroom, he joined Lisa and me at the table.

If possible he was even more pale, the circles beneath his eyes even darker. He seemed to be deteriorating, as if the center of him was slowly spinning apart and the rest of him imploding in on it.

"Are y'all any closer to catching him?" he asked. "I feel like I've been out of the loop lately. What's going on?"

I told him what Carla and Cody had told me about the abductions and torture without using their names.

His eyes grew wide, his gaunt face genuinely alarmed. "So it's a staff member? He's free? Just walking around out there somewhere?"

"That's most likely," I said. "Could be a work squad inmate but it's doubtful."

"I've actually felt somewhat safe when I wasn't at the prison," he said. "I've even been sleeping some at night." He shook his head, his breathing becoming even more erratic. "He knows who I am. He could come after me anytime."

"We're not going to let that happen," I said. "We're going to catch him very soon. We're getting closer and closer all the time."

He took in a deep breath and let it out very slowly, then did it again, and I could tell he was trying to regain his composure.

"Sorry," he said, still slightly out of breath. "I feel like such a . . . like he really did turn me into his little . . ."

"Don't be so hard on yourself. You've been through an awful experience. You're still traumatized. It's normal to be afraid."

We were quiet a few moments more as he seemed to continue to take control of his fear.

"Anything else?" he asked.

I wasn't sure if I should tell him any more but decided to. I'm of the school that it's always better to know.

"I'm okay," he said. "Really. It helps for me to know. It really does."

"I think the place he's taking them is close to the river," I said.

"Why?"

I told him what Cody said about hearing boats pass by.

"It can't be underground and close enough to the river for him to hear a boat pass by," he said. "It'd be full of water."

"That's true," I said. "Any place where a boat could pass by would be."

"Well, now, wait a minute," he said, his voice rising. "The river is low right now, the water table too. I guess it could . . . I remember reading something about a few bunkers built into the banks of the river during the Civil War. What if he's using something like that?"

I nodded. "Could be. Thanks. We'll check it out."

He stood and nodded at us. "Please let me know if . . . if anything new . . . if there's anything I need to know."

"I will."

"Thanks," he said, and returned to his table in the back.

"See a name on the top of the list who spends a lot of time on the river?" Lisa asked.

I glanced back at the list.

She tilted her head to the right a couple of times, indicating a table about ten feet away. Shane Bryant and Todd Sears sat in silence eating the Southern fried special designed to attract lunch customers like them who had no interest in anything except meat, potatoes, and vegetables.

Shane was on the list.

"He was in or around the medical building every time one of the rapes occurred, and he's always on the river," she said. "He could have found that Civil War bunker or whatever it is and turned into his own little rape room."

Merrill returned from the restroom shaking his head. "Guess what I just heard. Inspector found a shank with traces of blood on the tip hidden in Michael Jensen's duffle he left on the van when he escaped."

"When?" I asked. "Why'd it take so long?"

"That the kicker," Merrill said. "Was a while back. New warden told the inspector not to tell anyone—especially you or your dad."

"So he's the doer," Lisa said. "That's how the rapes are both inside and outside of the prison."

"We need to find out if the one outside of the prison took place after Jensen's escape and if there have been any others inside since he's been gone."

"I'll find out about the inside ones," she said. "You take the outside."

I nodded and looked back over at the bank. Uncle Charlie was still standing outside trying to get in. He was pulling on the right side door now, but it didn't budge either.

Scanning the restaurant, I spotted the bank president and a couple of the tellers. They were normally here at this time, and the bank usually stayed open.

"I'll be right back," I said, standing and dropping my napkin on the table.

"Something wrong?" Lisa asked.

By the time I was outside a small group of people had gathered around Uncle Charlie. They were pulling on the doors and cupping their hands around their faces as they pressed against the glass to see inside.

As I crossed the street an alarm began sounding and the small group was scattering, Uncle Charlie shuffling away as best he could.

Running toward the door I heard a vehicle speed up behind me and screech to a stop. I spun around hoping it was a deputy.

It wasn't.

It was an old mud-covered Ford truck. The driver was wearing a black ski mask, and holding a small handgun, which he had yet to point at anybody.

When I spun back around, two men in similar masks were unlocking the front doors of the bank and walking out. The large man in front held a shotgun in one hand and had a large black canvas bag draped over his opposite shoulder. The smaller man behind him had an identical bag and carried a handgun.

Reflexively I held up my hands.

I could hear crying and a few screams coming from inside the bank and the sound of a siren in the distance.

The man in the truck honked his horn and I turned my head toward him. He was motioning frantically to the two men coming out of the bank.

When I turned back toward them, the big man in front hit me on the side of the head with the butt of his shotgun. My knees buckled and I went down.

The pain in my head was so intense that I threw up and couldn't see for a moment.

As soon as I could I rolled over to get a better look at the robbers. They tossed the canvas bags in the back of the truck, jumped in the cab, and sped away.

I searched the bumper for the tag but there wasn't one. They had probably stolen the truck and removed the plates and would abandon it soon.

By the time I had gotten to my feet, people had emptied out of the Cajun Café and the other downtown businesses and were craning to see what was going on.

Within two minutes of the truck leaving, Jake, sirens screaming, lights flashing, sped by in the direction they had gone. He was alone in his patrol car and I motioned for him to stop so I could jump in and help, but he didn't see me.

I ducked into the bank to make sure everyone was okay.

They were.

The employees on duty at the time were all women, and though many of them were hysterical none of them had been injured in any way.

When I walked back outside, Merrill was pulling up.

"Somebody bitch slap me with they shotgun, I'm gonna wanna go after 'em."

"We got that in common," I said.

I rushed over as fast as my aching head would allow, dropped into the low car, and we took off after them.

Chapter Fifty-one

As usual Merrill's sporty black BMW looked as if he'd just driven it off a showroom floor. The dashboard glistened in the sunlight, its moist sheen seeming to soak up the rays. The carpet was spotless, the leather seats immaculate, and it smelled like a new car though he had owned it for a few years.

"Is there something blossoming in here?" I asked.

He smiled.

"All the little honeys like a ride to smell nice. Hell, most of 'em get one whiff and start taking off their panties."

I smiled. "Makes sense," I said. "Spring. Pollination. New life."

"Should try it in your new ride," he said.

He was driving fast, shifting often, passing anything that got in his way, but we had yet to see any sign of Jake or the truck.

After clicking on my seatbelt, I gently felt the growing knot on the side of my head.

"Anything broken?" Merrill asked.

"Just my head."

"Meant from getting whacked with the shotgun," he said. "Wasn't asking about preexisting conditions."

In the distance we could see Jake turning onto River Road, the sound of his siren barely audible.

Merrill smiled. "Dead end."

Four miles more and the road would dead-end into the river.

"Either these the dumbest bastards ever tried to rob a bank," he continued, "or they got a boat waiting."

After we turned onto River Road he sped up even more, taking took the numerous curves as if we were shooting a performance car commercial.

"Situation like this make you wish you didn't work at the prison," he said.

I nodded. I knew what he meant. Because it was a felony to have a weapon on state prison property—even locked in your car in the parking lot—the only weapons available were Merrill and his car.

"Won't be an issue if we flip over and roll down the highway several times," I said. "Or wrap around one of these big oak trees."

"How often a black man get to drive like this 'round here?" he said. "Hell, we usually get pulled over even when we just Sunday-afternoonin' it. 'Sides, I got this bitch 'cause it corners like it's on rails."

But he eased off the gas a bit and slowed down, especially around the curves.

As we neared the landing we heard gunshots and Merrill sped up again.

When we arrived, we found Jake crouched behind the open door of his patrol car, gun drawn, firing down into the river. We pulled up behind him, jumped out, and hunkered near the rear of his car.

He fired a few more times. Seemingly at nothing in particular. There was no return fire.

"Where are they?" I asked.

"Took off down the river," he said.

The bottom of his left pant leg was soaked in blood.

"What happened?"

"One of their shots hit the pavement and ricocheted into my calf," he said. "It's not bad."

"And why you shootin' the river?" Merrill asked.

"Trying to make sure they don't come back," he said.

Merrill looked at me, his eyes narrowed over a smirk. "Thought we raced down here to try to catch 'em."

Jake frowned and shook his head. "We were exchanging fire when they were trying to leave. I think I even got one of 'em. Anyway, they sped away so quickly, the bags of money fell out of the boat. I'm trying to keep them from coming back for them."

Merrill nodded. "Good work, Deputy."

I could hear sirens in the distance, faint, but growing.

"I've radioed in to let the others know they're headed down river," he said.

"All three of them?" I asked, looking around the landing.

"Yeah," he said. "Why?"

"Don't see their truck."

"They drove it off into the water," he said. "Over close to the boat launch."

"How long's it been since they've fired?" I asked.

"Why?"

"Wondering if it's safe to get the money and get you to the medical center."

"Should be," he said. "Let me get my shotgun and I'll cover you two while you get the money."

"Shee-it," Merrill said. "I know you the hero of the moment and all, but I ain't about to have you shootin' near my black ass. You could fuck up or just find it too temptin' and say you did."

"Then why don't you cover me," Jake said, "and I'll limp down there and get it and try not to bleed to death in the process."

"Much better plan," Merrill said with a big grin.

The sirens were getting closer. "If we wait just a minute," I said, "we'll have plenty of help and neither one of you will be in a position to have to resist the temptation to shoot the other."

Chapter Fifty-two

Pottersville State Bank was a red brick building with a front consisting mostly of dark plate glass. Its interior decor had changed many times over the years but the old black and woodgrain teller counters, desks, and tall standing tables had not.

While Jake was being treated at Pottersville Medical Center, and FBI agents were on their way, Dad, Fred Goodwin, Merrill, and I were sitting with Cathy Morris and Lonnie Potter in his office. Lonnie was the bank's president, a job consisting mostly of watching his family's money. Cathy, the executive who actually ran the bank.

The bank was closed, the blinds pulled. We were locked inside. The furniture of the lobby had been pulled back, and long sheets of plastic had been spread out in the middle of the floor. The recovered money was stacked on it, and four tellers—under the watchful eye of one of the board of trustees—were drying and counting it.

"With as small as we are and as electronic as banking has become," Lonnie was saying, "we just don't keep a lot of cash around anymore."

Lonnie Potter was a tall, thin, soft and soft-spoken man in his fifties. He had big blue eyes that were so wide he looked to be in a perpetual state of surprise, and his face was always red, as if from wind or razor burn.

"How much you think they got?" Dad asked.

"Oh, we know exactly," Cathy said.

Cathy Morris was a rigid, nervous single woman in her mid-forties, critical of most everyone and everything. She was so uncomfortable with herself, she made those around her uncomfortable—a defense mechanism she used to great advantage.

Dad raised his eyebrows. When Cathy didn't respond, he said, "How much?"

"Two hundred thousand," she said. "Exactly. They only took what was in the vault. They really seemed to know what they were doing."

"Really?" I asked, my voice full of surprise. "I didn't get that impression from their escape plan."

"And yet as I understand it," she said, "they have, in fact, escaped."

A boat Jake identified as the one the robbers used to escape was found about two miles down from the landing. If Jake had hit a man as he thought, the man hadn't bled in the boat. No blood, no prints, no trace evidence whatsoever had been found.

"So far," Dad said, "but there's only so many places they can hide out there. We'll find them."

"Like the inmate?" she asked.

Fred Goodwin laughed out loud.

"What made you think they knew what they were doing?" Dad asked, his voice firm and demanding.

"Well," she said, sitting a little straighter, "they came at the perfect time. We eat in two shifts—eleven to twelve and twelve to one. The hour from eleven to twelve has the least amount of people in the bank—and all women."

I glanced out at the women in the lobby drying and counting the recovered money. Two of them were recent high school graduates, two in their late thirties or early forties, none of them in shape. They did their work without talking, and I suspected it had more to do with the presence of Cathy Morris than concentration or post traumatic stress.

"Is that it?" Dad asked.

"Not even close," she said. "They came in through the back door, so no one passing by or in the shops across the street saw them. My office is back there, so they came in and got me first. They had me open the safe first. It's on a timer, so while they were waiting for it to open, they went in the lobby, got everybody to lie down on the floor, and locked the front doors."

"They had to know what they were doing," Lonnie said. "No question about it."

"Anything else?" Dad asked.

Cathy nodded. "They got the tellers out from behind the counter before they could push the alarm, and they didn't take any of the money from their drawers. That means they sacrificed over fifty thousand dollars, but it was the smartest thing they could've done. Every drawer has marked bills—not only that, but when you lift them up it sets off the alarm."

She paused for a moment, but it was obvious that she wasn't finished.

Lonnie's office held black-and-white photographs from the early days of the bank, color portraits of his wife and two daughters, and newspaper clippings from various significant Pottersville events, especially those involving the bank. Everything was professionally matted in expensive frames that matched each other and the office.

One look at his family and you knew they had money. I wasn't sure what it was exactly, but I suspected it had far less to do with their clothes and jewelry and the quality of the photographs than their features and the way they held themselves.

"The other thing is they were patient," she said. "It takes fifteen minutes for the safe to open. They seemed to know that. And they stayed cool while they waited for it. They were professionals. Never endangered anyone's life, never even raised their voices."

"Sounds like you were quite taken with them," Dad said.

Ignoring him, she added, "As far as I could tell, the only thing that they didn't count on was how little money there was in the safe. That's the only time they seemed the least bit upset or angry."

We were all quiet a moment.

"Recovering the money so fast has got to help with the primary tomorrow," Lonnie said to Dad.

He shrugged. "Maybe. Hard to say."

"Well, you've got my vote. And Jake has my admiration and appreciation."

"Did they sound local?" I asked.

Everyone turned and looked at me.

"Huh?" Cathy said, seemingly distracted.

"When the robbers talked," I said. "Did they have strong Southern accents? Did they sound like they were locals? Was there anything familiar about the way they sounded?"

She thought about it, looking up and squinting as she did. After a while, she began to nod. "They didn't say much, but they were definitely Southern."

"You got any thoughts?" Dad asked.

I nodded. "A few."

"Any you'd care to share?"

"They need to develop a little more first," I said.

He looked at me, frustration filling his face.

"If I had anything worth saying I would tell you," I said.

He frowned and sighed. "Okay."

Suddenly, there was additional tension in the room, and when he turned and looked back at the others, no one said anything.

In a moment, the head teller walked over nervously and stood in the doorway of Lonnie's office. She was a tall, big woman, but her sheepish demeanor made her seem small.

"Ms. Morris," she said.

Most professional women in small Southern towns are called *Miss* whether they are married or not. The fact that this woman, Cathy's age or older, was calling her *Ms.* had to be a result of Cathy demanding it.

"Yes," Cathy said, her voice cold and intimidating.

"We've got a problem," she said, as if it was her fault.

"What is it?"

"It's the money," she said.

"What about the money?"

"Are you absolutely certain there was two hundred thousand in the vault?"

Cathy looked at her in narrow-eyed, open-mouth shock, as if utterly appalled. "Absolutely certain."

"Then—" she began.

"What is it?" Cathy said. "Is some missing?"

"No, ma'am," she said.

"What then," Cathy said. "Spit it out."

"There's actually more," she said. "We got back extra."

Chapter Fifty-three

"What do you mean extra?" Cathy asked.

I slowly stood, trying not to be noticed.

"We got more money back than what was stolen," she said.

"Maybe we had more in the vault than we realized," Lonnie said. "It's possible."

It was possible for somebody like Lonnie maybe, but not Cathy. She would know precisely.

Ignoring Lonnie, Cathy said, "How much more?"

"They stole two hundred," she said, "and we got back two hundred and fifty."

"Two-fifty would include our teller drawers and everything," Lonnie said. "And they didn't take those."

I began slowly easing out of the office. I finally thought I understood what was going on, and it made me sick. My head ached, my throat constricted, and my stomach felt like I had been sucker punched.

"Where are you going?" Dad asked.

"I'm sorry," I said. "I don't feel good. I think I'm sick."

"Are you okay?" Goodwin asked.

"No," I said, "I'm sick. I'm sorry, but I've got to go lie down."

"We've got a cot in the conference room," Lonnie said.

I shook my head. "I think I better go home."

"What?" Dad asked in shock, his face full of alarm and something that might have been a look of betrayal. "Now? With all that's happening?"

"I'm sorry," I said. "I'll call you the moment I feel better."

"Okay," he said in a way that communicated that it was anything but.

Cathy stood and walked out to inspect the money. The others followed. Merrill broke off from the group and followed me out the front doors. One of the tellers was quick to come over and lock it behind us.

It was dusk now, the unseen sun illuminating the world with a diffused pastel softness.

"What is it?" Merrill said.

He knew me too well to buy what I had been selling inside.

"I'm not sure," I said.

"You need me?"

"I might."

"You know how to reach me," he said.

"Thank you," I said.

I didn't just mean for the offer of help or things he might do but for the things he wouldn't do—like press me or become petulant when I needed space.

He nodded as if he knew what I meant and it made me want to hug him, which, for his sake, I did not.

I drove as fast as I could to Pottersville Medical Center.

I found Jake in one of the small exam rooms alone. His left shoe off, the pant leg above it had been rolled up and a clean white bandage covered his wound.

When I caught his eye, I shook my head.

"What?" he said.

That one word held his usual disdain but he averted his

gaze and refused to meet my eye.

"Let's go," I said.

He started to protest but stopped when he finally locked eyes with mine.

I felt the urge to punch him, to close the space between us and just pound him until I felt better, but then tears formed in his big brown eyes, and I felt sorry for him.

The pity didn't replace my anger, just slipped in beside it and sat there, tempering, restraining.

"I need my boot," he said.

I looked around and found it. When I handed it to him he made no attempt to put it on, just held it as he pushed himself off the bed and hobbled toward the door. Alternating between wanting to help him and wanting him to hurt, I followed as he slowly limped over to the door and started down the hallway to the exit closest to the room.

We were near the exit when I heard the nurse rushing up behind us. She was a middle-aged gray-haired woman with an abrupt manner and a smoker's voice.

"What the hell are you doing?" she asked. "He can't—"

"Official police business," I said. "It's an emergency."

"I don't care what it is," she said. "He's got to stay off his leg."

"He will just as soon as I get him in the car," I said. "I promise."

"He's got to stay here," she said. "I'm going to call the doctor."

When she was gone, I said, "Think you can walk a little faster?"

He picked up the pace marginally and we made it out the door, across the side yard, and into the car before she returned with the doctor or anyone else.

As we drove off into the darkening evening, the street lamps beginning to come to life all around us, he said, "How much do you know?"

I shrugged. "No way of knowing without knowing how much there is to know," I said. "But here's what I think."

Chapter Fifty-four

"I think the plane I saw the day Michael Jensen escaped crashed into the river," I said. "I think it belonged to Air Ads Inc. and a guy called Junior was flying it. You guys were doing your search and rescue drills on the river and a plane crashes down on top of you. And when you go to search and rescue it you discover that the crash killed Junior, right? He was dead, wasn't he? Tell me y'all didn't help him along?"

"He was dead. I've never killed anyone—not even on duty."

"Y'all also discover that Junior's not one of the good guys. So instead of reporting the crash you take his money. Was it just money or something else too? Drugs, guns?"

"We only took his money," he said. "We saw an opportunity and took it. Hell, it happened so fast we didn't even really think about it."

I shook my head.

We drove through town, the lights inside houses blinking on, kids still out on bikes and skateboards, young women in groups of twos and threes power walking down the sidewalks in skimpy shorts, pumping their arms and working their mouths as they did.

"It was just money," he said. "He didn't need it anymore. We were going to divide it up."

"What the hell were you thinking, Jake?" I asked.

"Only one thing," he said. "Getting Mama a transplant."

For a moment I couldn't speak. The dumbest thing he had ever done might just have been for the best reason he'd ever done anything.

"That's why you were so certain Mom was going to get one."

He nodded.

"Your plan was to buy a black-market organ?" I asked.

He nodded again.

I shook my head. "Even if you actually could, which would be next to impossible, don't you realize somebody most likely would be murdered in order for her to get it?"

He didn't say anything.

"Where's the plane?"

"In the river," he said. "Almost dead in the middle, straight out from the cross that marks the spot where Taylor drowned."

"That's why it hasn't been found," I said, "why there was no debris field or fire. You're going to take me to it. Is one of the search and rescue boats still at the landing?"

He nodded.

"So after I recovered from Jensen jumping me," I continued, "I came to the landing with Dad to see if anyone saw a plane go down, and you guys, knowing exactly where it was and having just come from it, go and help me not find it."

He nodded again.

When we passed the bank I could see that Dad and the others were still inside. There was no sign that the FBI agents had arrived yet and I wondered how long it would be.

"The money was actually in the boat at the time," I said. "In your bags. That's why Goodwin was so anxious for everyone to unload their things to make room for me. It's why Todd was in no hurry to get the dogs and get searching for Jensen. It's why the equipment wasn't in your bags. The money was."

He didn't say anything, just stared straight ahead, wiping silent tears.

"Junior was dead when you got to the plane, wasn't he?" I asked.

He shrugged. "I think so," he said. "How'd you know?"

"What do you mean you think so?"

"I didn't actually go into the plane," he said. "Only Todd, Shane, and Kenny. But they said he was dead."

"He was the lynching victim, wasn't he?"

He nodded. "Think so. Haven't seen him but based on the description . . ."

"From the autopsy result we thought he'd been beaten to death before he was lynched, but actually he'd been in a plane crash. That's why he had water in his lungs too. Y'all hung him after he was already dead. But why? Why not just leave him in the plane?"

"We did," he said.

"What?"

"I swear," he said. "I swear to God, we only took the money. We left the pilot and everything else in the plane."

I thought about it.

"We couldn't've hidden him in a duffle bag," he said. "He wasn't in the boat when you got in with us—just the money. Why would we go back later, pull him out of the plane, and then lynch a dead man?"

As I turned onto River Road I couldn't help but feel the action carried a certain inevitability, as if everything that had been happening had been leading to this. It was as if the river had been silently beckoning us all along—whether to the cleansing of baptism or for its waters to turn crimson with our blood I could not tell. Perhaps only the river could.

"So who lynched him?" I asked.

"I don't know," he said. "Probably whoever killed Turtle and that SEAL guy."

"I figured it was you guys covering your crime," I said. "Figured they saw something—the plane, what you did, something, and y'all killed them."

He turned toward me in his seat, a slack-jaw stunned look on his face. "John," he said, his voice full of hurt and betrayal, "you think I'm a murderer? You think I could . . . All I did was take some piece of shit's drug money so I could save Mama. That's all. I ain't killed nobody. I can't believe you think I could."

I had wondered why he had been so willing to talk to me, so open and honest. He'd only been confessing to taking some drug money—and for a reason he knew I would understand and empathize with.

"You had nothing to do with the three murders?" I asked.

"I swear on Mama's life. I didn't kill anybody."

"Doesn't mean some of the other SAR members didn't," I said.

He nodded. "True. Thought they were gonna kill Sandy. He wouldn't take any of the money. Then he quit the team the next day. They thought he was gonna turn us in but I told 'em he wouldn't. He said he understood what I was doing and that he'd do the same thing for his mom. Told them to give me his share but they split it evenly between the five of us."

We were silent a moment and I thought about it some more.

"She's gonna die, John," he said.

"But you found out you couldn't get her a black-market organ because you had stolen counterfeit money," I said.

"How did you—"

"You staged the robbery today to exchange some of the funny money for some real," I said. "When I heard that there was more money returned than was taken, it brought to the surface all the other little things that had been bothering me about the whole thing, and I remembered Dad taking that secret service agent to the beach because a counterfeit bill was found down there."

"We got paranoid about the money," he said, "so we decided to float a little out there to see if anything was wrong with it. We did it over at the beach so it wouldn't be connected to us. If something was wrong with it everybody would think it came from a tourist. Hell, we were afraid it might be marked. Counterfeit never crossed our minds."

The winding road to the river was empty and dim, only an occasional streetlight and the half-moon to aid my headlights' attempt to cut through the low fog that crept out of the swamps on either side of us and hovered just above the road.

"Who did the bank job?" I asked. "Kenny and who?"

"Fred," he said. "How'd you know?"

"Kenny's size," I said. "I knew it wasn't Todd and Shane because they were in the restaurant when it happened. I knew it wasn't you because I saw you playing your part. I wondered how you got there so fast—and so far ahead of all the other cops. That was the plan, wasn't it? You weren't responding to an alarm or 911 call. And you never had a shoot-out with the robbers. They never even went in the river, did they?"

He shook his head.

"That's why the boat had no trace evidence at all," I said. "You guys cleaned it and left it where it was found before the robbery even began—just like the money. Drop the two bags of counterfeit money in the river and then tell your story when someone arrives."

He nodded. "Fred and Kenny took the real money out of the truck and into Kenny's car," he said. "Then drove the truck into the river."

"It wasn't a bad plan," I said, "but you guys only stole two hundred grand and you had already put two hundred and fifty in the other bags."

"We knew we couldn't exchange all of it," he said. "So—"

"How much is all of it?" I asked.

"Eight," he said. "We asked around and found out how much the bank kept on hand, how long it took for the safe to open. Hell, I already knew about the alarm and the marked money in the tellers' drawers."

"The bank keeps around two hundred and fifty," I said, "but that includes what's in the tellers' drawers."

"We fucked up," he said.

"Wasn't the first time," I said. "Did you shoot yourself in the leg?"

He nodded. "I didn't mean to," he said. "It was a stupid accident. Accidentally shot the asphalt and it ricocheted up and hit me. Hurt like hell. But helped my story. Least I thought it did."

"Did Turtle or the SEAL guy see you guys when you were at the plane?"

He shook his head. "I don't think so. Sure as hell didn't see them."

I thought about it for a minute, trying to assimilate what I had learned from him with what I already knew, trying to go with the shift in paradigm I was experiencing.

"You only have Todd, Shane, and Kenny's word about what was in the plane," I said. "Maybe Junior wasn't dead or maybe there was a lot more money in it than what they told you. Or other things."

"They could have gone back and—"

"Been seen by Turtle and the SEAL," I said, though something at the edges of my consciousness nagged me.

"But I still don't see why they brought the pilot up," he said.

"Maybe they didn't mean to," I said. "He could have floated up out of the plane while they were in it. They could have staged the lynching as a way to cover what y'all had done."

He nodded.

When we reached the landing I drove over to the search

and rescue boat and Jake's truck in the corner. There was no sign of anyone at the landing, though the vehicles of the deputies, FDLE agents, and game wardens searching for the bank robbers were scattered throughout.

"But that might not be it at all," I said. "Junior could still be in the plane."

"We need to find out," he said, "but with the way my leg is, I don't think I can dive."

"I can," I said.

Chapter Fifty-five

"When's the last time you dove?" he asked.

I turned off the car and cut the lights but didn't get out. I shrugged. "It's been a while."

"How many times have you since you got certified?"

Like most active people who lived near the Gulf of Mexico, I had taken a diving class and gotten certified as an open water diver. And though I really enjoyed diving—when my sinuses would let me do it pain free—I didn't have a boat or a dive buddy, and hadn't made much time for it in the two years since I had received my certification.

"Not many," I said.

"You're barely certified for open water," he said. "Your only experience has been in the Gulf. Not only is this a night dive around wreckage, it's in the river where visibility is usually near zero all the time anyway. There's gators, strange currents, and quicksand. Plus you don't have a partner."

"It'll be okay," I said. "As low as the river is, it can't be very deep. And you'll be right above me in the boat if I need help."

He shook his head. "Hell, no. I wouldn't be any help if you needed it. No."

"Jake we don't have a lot of options here. I'm trying to keep you out of prison."

He started to say something but stopped.

"I believe that you didn't have anything to do with the murders," I said. "And I understand why you did what you did. If we involve others, none of that's gonna matter."

Tears formed in his eyes again, and he blinked several times. "I'm sorry," he said. "I just thought if there was a chance to save her . . ."

"I know," I said. "You don't want to be in jail during her final days, do you?"

He shook his head.

"Come on," I said. "We need to get the boat launched and get out of here before the others come back."

As we neared the cross with Taylor's name on it, I recalled Merrill and me seeing Todd, Shane, Fred, and Kenny in this same spot the day we saw Jensen and stumbled onto the SEALs.

Had they gone back inside the plane or were they just making sure it still wasn't visible?

Jake cut the motor and let us drift into position. I took in a deep breath, held it a moment, then let it out slowly.

Those searching for the phantom bank robbers were several miles away. We appeared to be alone, though the loud nocturnal noises coming from the river swamps reminded us we weren't.

It was a dark night. There were no stars, and the half-moon, its reflection dancing on the black ripples of the river, provided little illumination. A light breeze blowing across the water and through the cypress, oak, and pine trees held in its comfortable currents the first hint of a North Florida fall.

Jake helped me prepare the equipment and put it on, insisting that I wear a wetsuit—something I hadn't done for my summer dives in the Gulf.

"It's not for temperature as much as protection."

The wetsuit was stiff and immobile and made it twice as difficult to put on the other equipment. It took a while to get ready and I began to become anxious about somebody discovering us.

In addition to the normal equipment—BCD, tank, regulator, depth and pressure gauges, mask, fins—Jake insisted that I wear gloves, take a diving knife, and carry a large light.

"Without the light you wouldn't see anything at all," he said. "With it you won't see much. It's going to be pitch black down there. Don't freak out."

"How deep is the plane?" I asked.

"Only fifteen feet," he said. "But this fifteen is far more dangerous than a-hundred-and-fifty-foot dives in the Gulf. Try to stay off the bottom—it can suck you under and not let go. Watch for trash, debris from the plane, snakes, gators. And don't go in the plane. Just look."

I gave him a mock salute and eased over to the edge of the boat, the extra weight and lack of mobility making it difficult. Sitting on the edge, I prepared to flip over backward into the dark water.

"Try your regulator," he said.

"Not until I get in the water and wash it off," I said. "Whose is it?"

He shrugged. "Just an extra. I'm sure we've all used it one time or another."

"I was really hoping not to catch a bad case of redneck," I said.

"Fuck you, you big sissy."

I smiled.

We fell silent a beat, and he said, "Moment of truth."

I nodded.

"John."

"Yeah?"

"Sorry about all this," he said. "I appreciate what you're

trying to do for me."

"Just be up here when I come back," I said.

"Just come back," he said.

I attempted to flip over backward, but only made it about halfway, my mask filling with water, my BC and tank twisting around, and the regulator getting knocked out of my hand.

"Goddamn," Jake said. "You're gonna die."

I started laughing. When I could, I said, "Just give me a minute to get my sea legs."

"You're in a fuckin' river, Einstein."

I took a minute to get everything back in place, wash off the regulator, test it, then I gave him the okay sign and began my descent.

Adjusting my buoyancy, I moved slowly down into the dark, wet underworld.

Jake had been right. It was pitch-black and scary. I tried to remind myself to take long, slow breaths, but my slightly panicked breaths were erratic and shallow. If I didn't get it under control soon, I was going to hyperventilate or drown.

The light illuminated only a small area right in front of it and then was subsumed by the darkness.

I had forgotten how strange the sounds were. All I could hear was the exaggerated sound of my breathing and the muffled echo liquidity of every sound.

After just five feet or so, I reinflated my BC to stop my downward motion, and took a moment to try to equalize the pressure in my head and stop the pain in my sinus cavities and ears. After a brief while of pinching my nose and blowing, and slowing down my breathing, I was ready to continue.

I deflated my BC and let the weight belt slowly pull me down, all the while trying not to think about what creatures were all around me, possibly preparing to strike.

Eventually my feet touched down on the top of the plane, which wobbled and shifted in the sand as I came to rest.

I inflated my BC enough to help me float and quickly took my weight off the plane.

Swimming down beside it, I held the light close to it, which confirmed it was the plane I had seen a couple of weeks back. It even had a small Air Ads Inc. logo on the tail. Coming around to the cockpit, I attempted to look inside, but the light was too weak, the river too dark, and all I saw was the light's reflection off the glass.

I pulled myself over to the door by using the plane itself, which continued to shift and settle in the push and pull of the currents. The door was slightly ajar, moving back and forth as the plane did.

I eased it open and leaned inside.

It was a small plane, barely big enough for two adults, and whatever had been in it, including Junior himself, was now gone.

I took another few minutes to look around the area, but could see so little even directly in front of me that it made it a complete exercise in futility. Finally, I gave up, and began my slow ascent toward the top.

Now that I was relaxed, I began to enjoy the dark, wet, womb-like embrace. As I floated I began to try to figure a way out for Jake that kept him out of prison and didn't cost Dad the election. Instead, the confirmations and revelations I had received from Jake took shape, and several elements of the case fell into place for me, and I began to better understand the murders and their meanings.

When I broke the surface of the river a minute or so later, Jake was gone.

Chapter Fifty-six

I pulled out the regulator, lifted the mask to the top of my head, and adjusted the BC so I could float and not have to tread water.

Just as I was about to turn around to see if Jake had drifted or changed positions for some reason, a light came on behind me. As I turned toward it I was blinded, unable to see who was shining it at me.

"We didn't leave anything down there, did we?"

I recognized the voice.

It was Todd. No doubt Shane was with him, and I wondered who else might be.

I closed my eyes, seeing spots as I did, and felt around behind me for the regulator hose. If I could pull the regulator toward me, deflate my BC, and stick the regulator in my mouth as I sank toward the bottom, I might be able to get away from them.

Before I could find the hose, I heard a shell being racked into the chamber of a shotgun.

"We want you stay up here with us," Shane said. "No need to be unsociable."

"Sorry," I said, without opening my eyes, "forgot my manners."

"Where's that big pussy brother of yours?" Todd asked.

"We know he brought you out here," Shane said. "Where'd he go?"

I attempted to shrug, but wasn't able to move my shoulders enough for it to qualify. "I figured y'all had him."

"We don't," Shane said.

Unless they were lying, and I couldn't figure why they would, Jake either left for some reason or something happened to him—a very real possibility on the river these days.

"I know how low an opinion of your brother you have," Shane said, "but he wouldn't just leave you down there. Hell, he's the reason you're still breathing. Been working his ass off trying to protect you and keep you out of all this."

"That mean he didn't help you kill my dog?"

"Of course he didn't," Todd said. "But the fact that you think he could shows you don't really know him."

"I told 'em we's killin' the wrong bitch," Shane said. "What's the name of that married bitch you been boning?"

I knew he meant Anna but I didn't say anything.

"Jake could need help," I said. "We should—"

"So?" Shane said.

"I thought he was one of your crew?" I said. "Thought you guys were brothers."

As I talked, I pretended to have to tread water, so I could reach down and grab the knife from the holster near the bottom of my right leg. Once I had the knife in my right hand, I opened my eyes again, avoiding the light, shading my eyes with my left.

"Fuck Jake," Shane said.

"If you don't care about Jake," I said, "then what about the money?"

"We've got the money," Todd said.

I shook my head. "You talking about the bags Kenny and Fred have?" I said. "That's more of the counterfeit money from the plane. Jake switched the bags with two others he had filled with another two hundred and fifty from the eight."

"Bullshit," Shane said.

Of course it was but it was the best I could do and I was hoping the details added to its credibility, which must have been what they did because I could hear a hint of doubt nibbling at the edge of his words.

"Call Kenny and ask him," I said, just making it up as I went along. "Ask him who loaded the money into the car while they put the truck in the river."

Not sure where that came from, but it didn't sound half bad. Even if they had a cell phone with them, it was doubtful they'd get any signal out here.

They had the drop on me and I was pretty sure they intended to kill me. I had to figure something out fast.

"That double-crossin' little cocksucker," Shane said.

"Jake's tryin' to save his mother's life," I said, attempting to add more credibility to my story. "He'd do anything. Even leave me out here alone. He's probably racing toward the hospital right now."

"Where would he take her?" Todd said.

"I have no idea," I said. "I'm not up on the black market. I honestly doubt Jake is either. He'll probably wind up killing her faster. I didn't say Jake was a genius. Just tellin' you what he's probably up to."

"And why are you doing that?" Todd asked.

His question had been sarcastic, but I answered as though it weren't.

"Because she's my mother too," I said. "If I thought there was any chance what he's tryin' would work, I'd be helping him. He needs to leave her alone, let her doctors do what they can. I wish you'd stop him. Besides, he double-crossed me too. Left me out here to die."

"Come on," Todd said. "Let's get him in the boat."

They trolled toward me, and when they got close enough to reach down for me, I ducked under the boat, deflated my

BC, and tried to find the regulator as I quickly sank toward the bottom.

Above me, the trolling motor started again, and shotgun pellets began piercing the water around me.

I was descending too fast without stabilizing, and my head began to hurt from the pressure building inside.

As I fell, I searched frantically for the regulator, dropping the knife and the light in the process.

Nearing the bottom again, I kicked my fins and partially inflated my BC. I couldn't be sure exactly how close I was to the riverbed, but if Shane was still firing, the rounds weren't making it down to where I was.

Finally able to find the hose, I pulled the regulator, put it in my mouth and willed myself to take deep, slow breaths.

When I had begun my quick descent, the mask had been on top of my head, and somewhere along the way, it had been knocked off. In terms of visibility, it was irrelevant, but the river water stung my eyes, and I wished I had it.

As soon as I was able I began to swim. If Todd and Shane had their dive equipment with them, they'd be suiting up right now and would be down here momentarily.

I had no idea which direction I was headed in. I was just trying to get as far away from them as fast as possible.

It occurred to me that if I stopped swimming and let the current carry me, I'd know I was headed down river.

So I did, eventually swimming with the current for a while then turning and heading toward land.

Unable to see anything—even my own hands out in front of me, I felt my way forward through the blackness, and I wondered how long it would be before I came in contact with a snake, gator, or turtle, or a log propelled by the oncoming current that would strike me and knock me unconscious, causing me to drown.

When I realized all Todd and Shane had to do to find me was follow the bubbles pouring from my regulator and popping up on the surface, I took in a deep breath, held it, and then changed directions.

I went with the current for a while again, then turned back toward shore, only breathing occasionally.

Now in addition to my head, my lungs and muscles ached, and I felt as if I wouldn't be able to go on any further, but just as I was about to give out, my hand felt the root system of a downed tree, and I knew I had made it to shore.

Using the root system for grip and the tree for cover, I came up slowly and quietly, and listened carefully as I wiped the river water from my eyes.

Suddenly the area around me was illuminated, and they were headed straight toward me in their boat, Shane firing the shotgun all around me.

They had me.

I was too close to shore, the water too shallow for me to disappear into it again.

They were coming at me fast as if they planned to just run over me, and there was nothing I could do.

Without warning, probably because it was running without lights and Todd and Shane's engine masked its sound, a boat shot out of nowhere. It rammed Todd and Shane's boat in the side, knocking them out of it and keeping it from hitting me.

A hand reached out of the darkness, grabbed my arm, and helped me roll into the boat.

"Come on, Chaplain," he said. "Let's get you out of here."

Chapter Fifty-seven

Looking up, I could make out the faint outline of Sandy Hartman in the moonlight.

"You okay?" he asked.

"Yeah," I said.

"I overheard them talking about taking care of a problem tonight," he said. "Figured it was me or you."

As he gunned the motor and took off, I slipped out of my BC, took my gloves and fins off, and sat up. Behind us, I could see Todd and Shane scrambling to get back in their boat, and I knew it wouldn't be long until they were coming after us.

The force of the wind on my wet body was cold and I began to shiver.

"You better get out of that wetsuit," he said.

Unfortunately I didn't have a whole lot on under it and I'd rather be cold than naked on the river.

"Shit," he said.

"What is it?"

"Here they come," he said. "This little boat won't outrun 'em. We'll have to find a place to hide."

"Any ideas?"

"Not far from here is a slough they call the River Sticks," he said. "Nobody goes back into it much. It's shallow and filled with fallen trees and limbs. It used to cut over to the Florida River, but a big oak tree has it completely blocked now."

"So if they find us, we'll be trapped."

"Unless we go ashore," he said.

"Any other options?"

"Not around here," he said.

"Okay," I said. "Let's do it."

We did.

Once in the slough he turned off the motor and began negotiating the narrow, obstacle-filled passage with a paddle and the trolling motor. The moon provided just enough light for me to see how appropriately named this small tributary was. Fallen trees from the banks extended out into the water, their craggy root systems thick and gnarled. Breaking through the surface at various spots throughout, the remnants of deadhead cypress trees were splintered and jagged.

As we ventured deeper and deeper down the small channel, the swamp on either side of us became thicker and thicker. My sense of claustrophobia increased with every stroke of the paddle or turn of the propeller. The trees, limbs, and roots scraped the sides and bottom of the boat, but never stopped it. With amazing skill and precision, Sandy adroitly steered the craft to safety.

Bringing the boat to rest against the huge fallen oak completely blocking the path, Sandy cut the trolling motor and we sat in silence, waiting. Within a few minutes we could hear Todd and Shane's boat approach the entrance of the slough, pass by, and continue down the river.

"What is it?" Sandy asked.

"What?"

"Somethin' wrong?" he asked.

"You mean besides the obvious?"

"Yeah."

"Like what?"

"I don't know," he said. "You just look . . . you're looking at me . . ."

"Where's Jake?" I asked.

"Huh?"

It was a risk, but one I had to take. Jake's life could very well depend on it.

"In your rape room in the old bunker? Is it close by? Has to be. No way you could have gotten through all those trees in the dark if you hadn't done it many, many times before."

The change that came over him as he sloughed off his public persona reminded me of taped interviews I had watched of people suffering from multiple personality disorder, and it was as if I were instantly, inexplicably with another person.

"I've worked with a lot of people who've done some evil things over the years," I said, "but there's very few I'd call evil."

"How'd you know?" he asked.

"Do you have Jake?"

He shook his head.

I thought about it.

"I'm just playing with you," he said. "I've got him."

He could be lying but I never believed Jake would leave me out there alone—not unless he was forced to.

Now that his mask was off and the man beneath could be seen, it was obvious that Sandy Hartman was detached, cold, and arrogant. He sat there patiently as if I posed no threat to him, as if I were completely in his control.

"Let's go see him," I said.

I wondered where he was, if he was really close by, and what Sandy had done with his boat.

"Tell me how you knew it was me," he said.

"The murders or the rapes?" I asked.

"Both," he said. "Start with the sex."

"It was brilliant to put the mark on yourself and pretend to be a victim," I said, "and you played the part to perfection— except for a few mistakes, which made a lot of little things add up for me."

He nodded, but didn't say anything. It was as if we were talking about something that only mildly interested but ultimately had nothing to do with him.

"You had access to the library and knew right where the Dalí was," I said. "I'm sure that there's a book of symbols that has the Mars and Venus and male and female signs as well. Not that you need a book for that."

"I wasn't familiar with the Dalí painting," he said. "See what you thought of it but it didn't provide any inspiration for me."

I nodded. "And while we're on the subject of the symbol and the act itself—they both speak of someone with a high degree of androgyny and sexual identity issues. You certainly fit that."

"That hurts my feelings," he said, his voice flat and insincere.

"What happened to you?" I asked. "Who made you a monster? Dad, step-dad, uncle?"

"I was born this way. Go back to the mistakes you said I made. What were they?"

To him this was all just a game—how he had fun—and all he seemed interested in was what he had done to betray himself.

"During the times you came to counseling with me," I said, "which I assume you did not only because you found it fun and exciting—and added dimension to the game, but so you could keep up with what we were finding out, you would periodically have toxic leaks."

"What?" he asked. "What is that?"

"The coarseness and profanity that spewed out of you," I said. "It didn't fit with the mask you were wearing—even considering what had happened to you. If something had actually happened to you."

He nodded and seemed to think about it, as if receiving feedback in an art class.

"The first day when you were telling me what the rapist had done to you," I said, "you got carried away. You were trying to gain my sympathy, to make sure I wouldn't suspect you, but you went too far. You told me after you did everything the rapist made you do, he still raped you."

"I knew that was a mistake the moment I did it," he said, "but I was caught up in the moment and went with it—what can I say? Hazards of the profession."

"The profession?"

"Acting."

I nodded.

"It was smart to use a shank to make it look like an inmate was responsible," I said, "but you just couldn't keep yourself from committing these crimes on the outside too."

"Didn't figure anyone on the outside would report it," he said.

"And they didn't."

"But of course you found out," he said.

"Hiding the shank in Jensen's duffle wasn't a bad idea, but there's no way he'd leave it on the van if he knew it was there, no way he wouldn't use it in his escape. Speaking of Jensen, after you raped him did you intercept a request to me from him?"

"The hell you know that?"

"He and his family mentioned to me about not helping him when he asked for it, but as far as I knew he never asked for it."

We were silent a beat.

"You're as good as everybody says you are," he said.

I shook my head. "If I were," I said, "my brother wouldn't be in your rape room and I wouldn't be out here in the middle of the swamp with you."

He laughed.

We were quiet another moment. In the distance we could hear Todd and Shane's boat motor. They were headed back in this direction.

"What about the other?" he asked, as if unable to call

them murders.

"Well once I realized the lynching victim was the pilot from the plane that went down, I figured it had to be you search and rescue guys," I said. "But once Jake convinced me it wasn't the whole group, then I got to thinking who it could be. Todd and Shane, even Fred were strong possibilities, but it came down to you for two reasons. The sexual component—you took Junior's clothes off and tied his hands to expose his genitals, you took the SEALs clothes off and strapped him down in a spread eagle position, and tried to make Turtle's look like an autoerotic asphyxiation accident—and since you bring your victims down here, it's possible Turtle or the SEAL died because they saw you doing that or found your bunker and didn't have anything to do with the plane or finding the money."

He nodded.

Todd and Shane were getting closer.

"Is Jake still alive?" I asked.

"I don't kill my sex partners," he said.

"He's not a partner yet," I said. "No way you had time to do anything 'cept grab him and hide his boat. Besides, this is different. We've seen you. Know you. And I suspect even though you started killing to cover up your other crimes, you're enjoying it too much to stop."

The moonlight glinted dully off his teeth as he smiled. "It's the most fuckin' amazing thing ever. Uh oh, was that a toxic leak?"

I didn't say anything.

"And so fuckin' easy. You can't imagine how little it takes to snuff somebody out."

I remained quiet.

"Come on," he said. "We've got to go."

Todd and Shane had turned onto the River Sticks, and would reach us in a matter of minutes.

"Why'd you get Junior out of the plane and hang him?" I asked.

"That the pilot? I went back to see if those redneck cocksuckers had lied about what was inside the plane, and the son of a bitch slipped out and floated to the surface."

I nodded.

"Now come on," he said. "Time to say goodbye to your brother."

Chapter Fifty-eight

As we stood, he swung the paddle around and hit me on the side of the head. The blow was on the opposite side of the one from the butt of the shotgun.

The paddle had far less mass and much more velocity.

My ear felt as if it had been knocked off my head, my knees buckled, and I fell out of the boat and into the water, the jagged end of a branch scratching the left side of my body as I did.

In an instant he was on me, holding my head beneath the surface of the water, choking me.

I tried to fight back, but after both blows to the head, the dive, and all the swimming, I had nothing left. I would have died right then and there if he had wanted me to.

But, of course, he had other plans for me, and he wouldn't kill me until he had finished playing.

Eventually he pulled me up onto the bank, cuffed my hands with flex cuffs, and taped my mouth shut with duct tape. He then dragged me up on the top of a small ridge and left me there, and when Todd and Shane arrived I knew why.

I was his audience.

I moved and struggled against my restraints but couldn't break free. When I tried to yell it came out as a muffled whimper. Nothing I did got their attention as they pulled up beside Sandy's boat.

Finally as a last resort I rolled down the small incline

toward them. As soon as they saw me they began firing. Several of the rounds pocked the clay and sand of the bank beside me but all of them managed to miss me.

When I reached the bottom and stopped rolling, both men took better aim, carefully eyeing down the sites of their barrels at me.

I tried frantically to signal them with my eyes and muffled grunts, but they didn't pay any attention—didn't even pause to wonder why I was bound and gagged, just wanted me dead.

Todd had a handgun, Shane, a rifle, and as trained, each man took in a small breath, let it out slowly, and began to squeeze the trigger. But before they could, Sandy came up out of the water behind them and shot Shane in the back of the head, grabbed Todd by his hair, pulled his head back, and slit his throat.

Shane fell forward, Todd backward, both of them half in and half out on either side of the boat. I closed my eyes, squeezing them hard against the horror I had just seen.

"Come on," Sandy said, as he pulled me up. "Let's go. I'll clean up this mess later."

He pulled me into the swamp, smearing Todd's blood on the arm of my wetsuit as he did.

"See how easy that was," he said. "Told you."

The farther we walked, the thicker the swamp became.

We had to step over fallen trees, around small tributaries fed by the slough. The soft dive boots I wore were no match for the terrain, and small sticks and thorns began cutting and tearing my feet.

"Don't slow down," he said, jerking my arm. "We're almost there. Jake's waiting for you. You won't believe the things I'll make him do. Of course it won't be anything compared to what you're going to do."

In another minute or so he stopped pulling on me and

I could see a mound of earth in front of him. Brushing away pine, straw, leaves, and removing propped-up branches, he exposed an old wooden door on two rusted hinges.

The door creaked as it opened. Turning and grabbing me, he shoved me inside.

I fell face first onto the muddy floor of a small hollowed-out place in the earth. It was dark but I could tell that it was tiny and I was not alone. I could hear muffled whimpering sounds and I knew that Jake's mouth was taped shut too.

Sandy came in with a light and closed the door behind him.

Jake's eyes grew wide with fear and he looked over at me, pleading.

When he saw I was cuffed too all hope drained from his face.

Jake was facedown on an old wooden table, his hands and feet stretched out by ropes that disappeared beneath it. He was naked, the paleness of his exposed skin adding to his vulnerability and violation.

Thankfully that was the only violation so far. There was no way Sandy had time to do anything else and get back to pick me up when he did.

The room wasn't the torture chamber I had imagined it to be. More than anything it was an empty underground tomb. The boards of the walls were ancient and splintered, the dirt behind them breaking through. The beams holding up the ceiling looked brittle, the boards they were supporting, wet and rotten. It wouldn't be long before this wasn't a room at all.

Snatching me up and shoving me into the corner, Sandy bound my feet together at the ankles, then walked over to Jake and untied his right hand.

"Wakey wakey, Jakey Jakey," he said in a demented, child-like voice. "Daddy wants to play."

Pulling out his gun and knife, Sandy turned to me, held

them up, and said, "Which do you think is more menacing?"

I tried to say something but the tape prevented it.

"You're right," he said. "We'll start with the knife, then switch to the gun if we don't get the desired results. You're good at this, John. A real natural."

I looked around the room and tried to think about how I might attack him or what I could use for a weapon. There was nothing and as weak as I was, and with my hands and feet bound, I wasn't much of a threat. Still, I had to try. I crouched there in the damp earth waiting for the best time.

Sandy leaned over, put the knife to Jake's throat, and began to whisper in his ear.

Slowly, Jake moved his hand around back behind him. I slowly eased up, preparing to strike.

Suddenly, Jake's free hand shot up and grabbed Sandy's wrist. I jumped, hopped, and fell as fast and as hard as I could and crashed into Sandy, knocking him away from Jake and onto the floor against the wall, landing on top of him in the process.

One of the boards in the wall snapped and dirt came pouring in on top of us.

As I tried to get to my feet, Jake tried to untie himself with his free hand. Neither of us were successful. Unable to stand, I felt around the dirt for the knife Sandy had dropped, but couldn't find it.

Pulling his knees up to his chest, he kicked me off of him with both feet and I flew halfway across the room. When he stood up, he was holding the gun. He stepped over to Jake, grabbed his free hand, and shot straight through it.

Jake screamed so loudly the tape around his mouth couldn't keep it in.

Sandy then turned and moved toward me.

When he reached me he pressed the muzzle of the gun into my forehead, the hot barrel burning my skin. I snatched back.

"This'll only hurt a split second," he said. "I promise.

Sorry you can't stay and play, but it's obvious you really don't want to."

Before he could pull the trigger, the door opened, and he turned in shock to see who it was.

No one was there. He turned and stared up through the doorway, a puzzled expression on his face.

Suddenly Michael Jensen flew through the door and tackled Sandy, knocking him to the ground. Sitting on top of him, Jensen brought up his large hunting knife and began a frenzied attack.

Sandy tried to bring up his gun and fire but wasn't able. The blows were too severe.

Jensen stabbed him for a long time—long, long after he was dead.

Eventually, having slain the dragon, he got up and walked out of the room without saying a word.

Chapter Fifty-nine

$\mathbf{A}$ Pottersville tradition on election day is for the county commissioners to post the results in front of Potter State Bank.

In the evening, the sun sinking somewhere in the unseen distance, folks gathered and waited to see not just who won but how everyone did.

Everyone was connected to everyone else in some way, most in many.

The following evening, the day of the primary, I pulled into the bank parking lot, got out, and joined the small crowd of onlookers. At the front of the crowd, the county commissioners somehow managed to look imminently important and truly humble as they watched as the votes were tallied and the results written on large dry-marker boards on stands constructed by inmates.

No one seemed to notice the crime scene tape spread across the bank's doors.

Through the crowd I spotted Cody and Carla sitting on his tailgate in the parking lot, and I walked over to them.

Carla stood up and hugged me as I neared. I hugged her back far more intensely than I normally did. I was happy to see her, thankful to be alive, glad I had awakened from the most recent nightmare.

When I released her, she gently touched the bruising on

my face. "What happened?"

When she sat back down beside Cody, I said, "The monster is dead."

Carla gasped.

Cody's eyes grew wide and he looked as if he wanted to believe it were possible but just couldn't.

"The guy who . . ." Cody began.

I nodded.

"Who was it?" he asked. "Do I know him?"

"You'll hear all about it in a day or two," I said. "I just wanted you to know now."

"And you're sure?" he asked.

"Positive," I said.

Cody's eyes moistened and he blinked back tears. Carla took his hand.

When I turned toward the crowd the sheriff's race results had been posted and people were congratulating Dad—even those who didn't vote for him. All he had won was the opportunity to run in the general election, but that was more than he thought he might get a few days ago. He looked relieved.

After leaving the river the night before I had taken Jake to the emergency room in Panama City. Once the wound in his hand had been treated we went up to Mom's room and spent several hours with her, during which time I told Mom how much I loved her but that Jake loved her more.

Eventually we called Dad and he met us there. We told him what had happened and we devised a plan that would keep Jake out of jail and Dad in office. We would turn in all the money—both from the bank and the plane—and say that Jake was working undercover for the sheriff's department. I had taken some time to think about it, to weigh what I was about to do, and decided it was the thing to do. Since then I had reexamined my motives and choices and actions and had reached the same conclusion. If Jake had hurt or killed anyone things would be different, but as it was all he did was make some stupid choices with some good intentions. He was just a boy trying to save his mother—something I could certainly understand.

And though everyone had agreed to keep the deaths and arrests concealed until after the election, Jake, Dad, and I had told our stories to FDLE and the FBI, and it looked as if they believed us. It would be a while before everything was over, but I suspected that what we did wouldn't just keep Jake out of jail but save his life, and might actually be the thing that won Dad reelection.

Once the results were posted, most people slowly scattered, rushing off to pick up their kids from football, volleyball, or soccer practice, or to cook supper and eat with their families.

Unlike usual I was in no hurry to leave. I had no place to go really, and what I was witnessing was a small-town way of life that was as valuable as it was vulnerable.

"Congratulations," I said to Dad when he walked up.

"Thanks," he said. "And thank you for what you did for Jake—and me. I really appreciate it, son."

I nodded.

"Still haven't found Jensen," he said. "Search will intensify now. Won't be long."

"He saved our lives," I said.

He nodded.

We were silent a moment, him shaking the hands of the people who walked by and congratulated him.

"You're not gonna charge him, are you?"

He shook his head. "There'll be some pressure to because of how violent and excessive he was, and some'll say I'm not charging him because you and Jake were involved, but no, I'm not. I'm calling it what it was. Self-defense."

I nodded. "Heard Fred dropped out of the race," I said.

He smiled.

"Should make the general election a lot easier."

"Will."

"I'm looking into the disappearance of R. L. Jenkins," I said. "Just wanted you to know."

"Who?"

"The minister from Marianna Merrill saw lynched when he was little."

He nodded. "Didn't figure you'd wait. I'll help as much as I can. When the election is over . . . we'll really dig into it . . . providing you don't have it solved by then."

We fell quiet a moment.

A few more people came by. He heard a few more congratulations and shook a few more hands.

"I've got to get back over to the office to meet with FDLE and the FBI," he said. "We're going to schedule a press conference for later tonight. Wanna come?"

I shook my head. "No thanks."

"Can't blame you," he said. "They'll never know all you did. How relentless you were—as usual, how you put things together and figured things out that no one else would have. How you saved lives—and souls," he added, nodding over toward Cody and Carla. "But I do. I know it all. And no dad could be more proud of his son than I am of you."

My eyes stung and I had to take in a deep breath to gain control of myself.

"Thank you," I said.

He extended his hand not as a dad but as a man shaking the hand of another man he admired and respected, and I shook it.

As he walked away, I couldn't remember him ever saying anything to me that meant any more than that.

I was overwhelmed.

Leaving the bank parking lot, I walked over to the small lakeside park next to it and sat down on one of the benches.

Sitting there alone in the evanescent evening, I thought about all that had happened and my part in it. I thought about my friends and coworkers and whispered a prayer for Merrill again. I thought about my family and my life and I gave thanks. I thought about Mom, her dying, her death, and knew that she wouldn't be the only one dying before she wanted to. We all would. All we could do was live while we had life in our lungs, do the best we could, enjoy the journey, walk humbly, act nobly, and be the best version of ourselves we could possibly be in any given moment.

I thought what a fine thing it is to be alive and I was filled with hope and thought my dark night of the soul might be about to break for the dawn, but even if it wasn't I felt somehow I would be okay.

I found myself accepting what was instead of futilely fighting against it, embracing everything—even having to give up of Anna—and I felt peaceful.

Later, in full evening, when everyone had gone back to their lives, back to their loved ones, I still sat alone.

Across the way I saw Anna pull up and park next to my car.

Searching around until she found me, she walked over without ever even glancing at the election results.

She sat down on the bench beside me and a long moment passed before either of us spoke.

Eventually she said, "Birth control pills make me sick. I mean really mess me up, my hormones, my . . . everything. I can't take them."

I looked at her. I knew she had a reason for telling me so I waited.

"Chris confessed to me last night that he's been poking holes in his condoms in hopes of making me pregnant. Said he was afraid of losing me. Wanted some insurance. Something to bind me to him forever."

I took her hand.

"Can you believe that?" she asked.

"Sure," I said.

She turned and looked at me, studying my face. It was obvious I hadn't given her the response she'd been expecting.

"It was a dishonest act of desperation," I said. "It shows cowardice and control issues and a level of obsession I wouldn't expect from Chris, but I can certainly understand it. I wouldn't be surprised by anything you'd inspire a man to do."

"Would you do it?" she asked.

I didn't answer.

"Would you?"

I shook my head. "No." I said. "I wouldn't."

"What's that line about honor you're always quoting?"

"'Yet this inconstancy is such . . . as thou too shalt adore . . . I could not love thee, dear, so much . . . loved I not honor more.'"

She nodded appreciatively, gazing out over the lake.

"Said he did it so when I found out he'd had an affair I might not leave him."

"Oh, Anna, I'm so sorry," I said. And I really was.

"What should I do?" she asked.

"I can't tell you that."

"I left him," she said.

With those words my heart did something it hadn't done in a while. It leapt.

"I'm not going back."

"You're not just acting out of anger or . . ."

She shook her head. "I'm really not. All the things he's done are just symptoms."

I nodded slowly, thinking about it, trying to contain myself.

"We should've never married, never been together in the first place. I've only stayed out of obligation and some misguided notion of honor."

I nodded.

She turned and looked at me, our longing eyes locking.

"I want you to think about something and answer me honestly," she said. "Don't worry about hurting my feelings or discouraging me. I want the truth. All I have room for in my life now is truth."

"Sure," I said.

"Do you think there's a man out there who can love me even though I'm carrying another man's child?" she asked. "Even though I'm a damaged, soon-to-be-divorced, soon-to-be-single mom with bumps and bruises and baggage? I know it'd be an awful lot to ask of a man. I know it'd take someone very, very special to love me and my baby the way we deserve. And I know it won't be easy to find such a person. I realize that. I mean . . . So all I guess I'm really asking is if . . . if you think such a person exists."

"I do."

At the author's request, this book has been typeset in Garamond using a ragged right margin. The author feels this non-uniform, lack of right side alignment best fits his aesthetic. We agree.

About the Author

Multi-award-winning novelist, Michael Lister, is a native Floridian best known for literary suspense thrillers and mysteries.

The Florida Book Review says that "Vintage Michael Lister is poetic prose, exquisitely set scenes, characters who are damaged and faulty," and Michael Koryta says, "If you like crime writing with depth, suspense, and sterling prose, you should be reading Michael Lister," while Publisher's Weekly adds, "Lister's hard-edged prose ranks with the best of contemporary noir fiction."

Michael grew up in North Florida near the Gulf of Mexico and the Apalachicola River in a small town world famous for tupelo honey.

Truly a regional writer, North Florida is his beat.

In the early 90s, Michael became the youngest chaplain within the Florida Department of Corrections. For nearly a decade, he served as a contract, staff, then senior chaplain at three different facilities in the Panhandle of Florida—a unique experience that led to his first novel, 1997's critically acclaimed, POWER IN THE BLOOD. It was the first in a series of popular and celebrated novels featuring ex-cop turned prison chaplain, John Jordan. Of the John Jordan series, Michael Connelly says, "Michael Lister may be the author of the most unique series running in mystery fiction. It crackles with tension and authenticity," while Julia Spencer-Fleming adds, "Michael Lister writes one of the most ambitious and unusual crime fiction series going. See what crime fiction is capable of."

Michael also writes historical hard-boiled thrillers, such as THE BIG GOODBYE, THE BIG BEYOND, and THE BIG HELLO featuring Jimmy "Soldier" Riley, a PI in Panama City during World War II (www.SoldierMysteries.com). Ace Atkins calls the "Soldier" series "tough and violent with snappy dialogue and great atmosphere . . . a suspenseful, romantic and historic ride."

Michael Lister won his first Florida Book Award for his literary novel, DOUBLE EXPOSURE. His second Florida Book Award was for his fifth John Jordan novel BLOOD SACRIFICE.

Michael also writes popular and highly praised columns on film and art and meaning and life that can be found at www.WrittenWordsRemain.com.

His nonfiction books include the "Meaning" series: THE MEANING OF LIFE, MEANING EVERY MOMENT, and THE MEANING OF LIFE IN MOVIES.

Lister's latest literary thrillers include DOUBLE EXPOSURE, THUNDER BEACH, BURNT OFFERINGS, SEPARATION ANXIETY, and A CERTAIN RETRIBUTION.

CPSIA information can be obtained at www.ICGtesting.com
Printed in the USA
LVOW13*0931260114

371015LV00003B/25/P

9 781888 146394